Selected Stories by

JACK LONDON

Books in this Series:

Selected Stories by O. Henry

Selected Stories by Anton Chekhov

Selected Stories by Guy de Maupassant

Selected Stories by Mark Twain

Selected Stories by Edgar Allan Poe

Selected Stories by Rudyard Kipling

Selected Stories by Saki

Selected Stories by Oscar Wilde

Selected Stories by Honoré de Balzac

Selected Stories by Charles Dickens

Selected Stories by D.H. Lawrence

Selected Stories by H.G. Wells

Selected Stories by Jack London

Selected Stories by Joseph Conrad

Selected Stories by Leo Tolstoy

Selected Stories by Sir Arthur Conan Doyle

Selected Stories by
JACK LONDON

RUPA

Published by
Rupa Publications India Pvt. Ltd 2014
7/16, Ansari Road, Daryaganj
New Delhi 110002

Sales Centres:
Allahabad Bengaluru Chennai
Hyderabad Jaipur Kathmandu
Kolkata Mumbai

ISBN: 978-81-291-3253-6

First impression 2014

10 9 8 7 6 5 4 3 2 1

Printed at Shree Maitrey Printech Pvt. Ltd., Noida

CONTENTS

INTRODUCTION

John Griffith 'Jack' London (12 January 1876–22 November 1916) was an American author, journalist and social activist. He was born in San Francisco to an unmarried mother, Flora Wellman, who came from a wealthy background. Because of Flora's illness, young Jack was raised by an ex-slave. Later, in 1876, Flora married John London, a partially disabled Civil War veteran.

London was a strong supporter of unionization, socialism and the rights of workers, and wrote about these issues in his fiction and non-fiction.

He was also one among the many writers to have worked in the movie industry and see his novels made into films. His novel, *The Sea Wolf* was the basis of a full-length American movie. He was also one of the first celebrity writers to endorse commercial products in advertisements.

- 'A Piece of Steak' is a poignant story of an aging boxer dealing with poverty and coming to terms with the fact that in his profession, one is invincible only as long as one is young.
- 'Brown Wolf' is the tale of Walt and Madge, who get a stray dog and name him Wolf. One day, Wolf's old master returns. The choice now lies with Wolf on who does he want to stay with.
- 'Flush of Gold' is the story of a beautiful woman who has been waiting for a dead man for nine years.

- 'Four Horses and a Sailor' is about a man who has never rode a horse but sets out on a journey with four horses.
- Abandoned by his friend in the wilderness, 'Love of Life' is the tale of a man who survives hunger, inclement weather and wild animals.
- 'A sailor is born, not made,' says the narrator of 'Small-boat Sailing', as he recounts his valorous experience of being at sea.
- 'The Handsome Cabin Boy' is a delightful story of a bet between two friends, a beautiful woman and a surprising turn of events.
- 'The Law of Life' is a poignant story of an old Indian chief Koskoosh, who is left behind as his tribe moves in search of food and shelter, and whose son has his family to take care of.
- 'The Pen' is the tale of a prisoner and the unusually colourful and active life he and fellow prisoners lead in Erie County Pen.
- 'The Son of the Wolf' is the story of love against insurmountable odds.
- 'The Wife of a King' is a touching story of an Indian woman, Madeline, whose husband leaves her in order to find a white woman, while Madeline strives to become more 'white'.

1

A PIECE OF STEAK

With the last morsel of bread Tom King wiped his plate clean of the last particle of flour gravy and chewed the resulting mouthful in a slow and meditative way. When he arose from the table, he was oppressed by the feeling that he was distinctly hungry. Yet he alone had eaten. The two children in the other room had been sent early to bed in order that in sleep they might forget they had gone supperless. His wife had touched nothing, and had sat silently and watched him with solicitous eyes. She was a thin, worn woman of the working-class, though signs of an earlier prettiness were not wanting in her face. The flour for the gravy she had borrowed from the neighbour across the hall. The last two ha'pennies had gone to buy the bread.

He sat down by the window on a rickety chair that protested under his weight, and quite mechanically he put his pipe in his mouth and dipped into the side pocket of his coat. The absence of any tobacco made him aware of his action, and, with a scowl for his forgetfulness, he put the pipe away. His movements were slow, almost hulking, as though he were burdened by the heavy weight of his muscles. He was a solid-bodied, stolid-looking man, and his appearance did not suffer from being overprepossessing. His rough clothes were old and slouchy. The uppers of his shoes were too weak to carry the heavy resoling that was itself of no recent date.

And his cotton shirt, a cheap, two-shilling affair, showed a frayed collar and ineradicable paint stains.

But it was Tom King's face that advertised him unmistakably for what he was. It was the face of a typical prize-fighter; of one who had put in long years of service in the squared ring and, by that means, developed and emphasized all the marks of the fighting beast. It was distinctly a lowering countenance, and, that no feature of it might escape notice, it was clean-shaven. The lips were shapeless, and constituted a mouth harsh to excess, that was like a gash in his face. The jaw was aggressive, brutal, heavy. The eyes, slow of movement and heavy-lidded, were almost expressionless under the shaggy, indrawn brows. Sheer animal that he was, the eyes were the most animal-like feature about him. They were sleepy, lion-like—the eyes of a fighting animal. The forehead slanted quickly back to the hair, which, clipped close, showed every bump of a villainous-looking head. A nose, twice broken and moulded variously by countless blows, and a cauliflower ear, permanently swollen and distorted to twice its size, completed his adornment, while the beard, fresh-shaven as it was, sprouted in the skin and gave the face a blue-black stain.

All together, it was the face of a man to be afraid of in a dark alley or lonely place. And yet Tom King was not a criminal, nor had he ever done anything criminal. Outside of brawls, common to his walk in life, he had harmed no one. Nor had he ever been known to pick a quarrel. He was a professional, and all the fighting brutishness of him was reserved for his professional appearances. Outside the ring he was slow-going, easy-natured, and, in his younger days, when money was flush, too open-handed for his own good. He bore no grudges and had few enemies. Fighting was a business with him. In the ring he struck to hurt, struck to maim, struck to destroy; but there was no animus in it. It was a plain business proposition. Audiences assembled and paid for the spectacle of men knocking each other out. The winner took the big end of the purse. When Tom King faced the Woolloomoolloo Gouger, twenty years before, he knew that the Gouger's jaw was only four months healed after having been broken in a Newcastle bout. And he had played for that jaw and broken it again in the ninth round, not because he bore the Gouger any ill-will, but because that was the surest way to put the Gouger out and win the big end of the purse. Nor had the Gouger borne him any ill-will for it. It was the game, and both knew the game and played it.

Tom King had never been a talker, and he sat by the window, morosely silent, staring at his hands. The veins stood out on the backs of the hands, large and swollen; and the knuckles, smashed and battered and malformed, testified to the use to which they had been put. He had never heard that a man's life was the life of his arteries, but well he knew the meaning of those big, upstanding veins. His heart had pumped too much blood through them at top pressure. They no longer did the work. He had stretched the elasticity out of them, and with their distention had passed his endurance. He tired easily now. No longer could he do a fast twenty rounds, hammer and tongs, fight, fight, fight, from gong to gong, with fierce rally on top of fierce rally, beaten to the ropes and in turn beating his opponent to the ropes, and rallying fiercest and fastest of all in that last, twentieth round, with the house on its feet and yelling, himself rushing, striking, ducking, raining showers of blows upon showers of blows and receiving showers of blows in return, and all the time the heart faithfully pumping the surging blood through the adequate veins. The veins, swollen at the time, had always shrunk down again, though not quite—each time, imperceptibly at first, remaining just a trifle larger than before. He stared at them and at his battered knuckles, and, for the moment, caught a vision of the youthful excellence of those hands before the first knuckle had been smashed on the head of Benny Jones, otherwise known as the Welsh Terror.

The impression of his hunger came back on him.

'Blimey, but couldn't I go a piece of steak!' he muttered aloud, clenching his huge fists and spitting out a smothered oath.

'I tried both Burke's an' Sawley's,' his wife said half apologetically.

'An' they wouldn't?' he demanded.

'Not a ha'penny. Burke said—' She faltered.

'G'wan! Wot'd he say?'

'As how 'e was thinkin' Sandel ud do ye tonight, an' as how yer score was comfortable big as it was.'

Tom King grunted, but did not reply. He was busy thinking of the bull terrier he had kept in his younger days to which he had fed steaks without end. Burke would have given him credit for a thousand steaks—then. But times had changed. Tom King was getting old; and old men, fighting before second-rate clubs, couldn't expect to run bills of any size with the tradesmen.

He had got up in the morning with a longing for a piece of steak, and the longing had not abated. He had not had a fair training for this fight. It was a drought year in Australia, times were hard, and even the most irregular work was difficult to find. He had had no sparring partner, and his food had not been of the best nor always sufficient. He had done a few days' navvy work when he could get it, and he had run around the Domain in the early mornings to get his legs in shape. But it was hard, training without a partner and with a wife and two kiddies that must be fed. Credit with the tradesmen had undergone very slight expansion when he was matched with Sandel. The secretary of the Gaiety Club had advanced him three pounds—the loser's end of the purse—and beyond that had refused to go. Now and again he had managed to borrow a few shillings from old pals, who would have lent more only that it was a drought year and they were hard put themselves. No—and there was no use in disguising the fact—his training had not been satisfactory. He should have had better food and no worries. Besides, when a man is forty, it is harder to get into condition than when he is twenty.

'What time is it, Lizzie?' he asked.

His wife went across the hall to inquire, and came back.

'Quarter before eight.'

'They'll be startin' the first bout in a few minutes,' he said. 'Only a try-out. Then there's a four-round spar 'tween Dealer Wells an' Gridley, an' a ten-round go 'tween Starlight an' some sailor bloke. Don't come on for over an hour.'

At the end of another silent ten minutes, he rose to his feet.

'Truth is, Lizzie, I ain't had proper trainin'.'

He reached for his hat and started for the door. He did not offer to kiss her—he never did on going out—but on this night she dared to kiss him, throwing her arms around him and compelling him to bend down to her face. She looked quite small against the massive bulk of the man.

'Good luck, Tom,' she said. 'You gotter do 'im.'

'Ay, I gotter do 'im,' he repeated. 'That's all there is to it. I jus' gotter do 'im.'

He laughed with an attempt at heartiness, while she pressed more closely against him. Across her shoulders he looked around the bare room. It was all he had in the world, with the rent overdue, and her and the kiddies. And he was leaving it to go out into the night to get meat for his mate and cubs—not like a modern working-man going to his machine grind, but in the old, primitive, royal, animal way, by fighting for it. 'I gotter do 'im,' he repeated, this time a hint of desperation in his voice. 'If it's a win, it's thirty quid—an' I can pay all that's owin', with a lump o' money left over. If it's a lose, I get naught—not even a penny for me to ride home on the tram. The secretary's give all that's comin' from a loser's end. Goodbye, old woman. I'll come straight home if it's a win.'

'An' I'll be waitin' up,' she called to him along the hall.

It was full two miles to the Gaiety, and as he walked along

he remembered how in his palmy days—he had once been the heavyweight champion of New South Wales—he would have ridden in a cab to the fight, and how, most likely, some heavy backer would have paid for the cab and ridden with him. There were Tommy Burns and that Yankee nigger, Jack Johnson—they rode about in motor cars. And he walked! And, as any man knew, a hard two miles was not the best preliminary to a fight. He was an old un, and the world did not wag well with old uns. He was good for nothing now except navvy work, and his broken nose and swollen ear were against him even in that. He found himself wishing that he had learned a trade. It would have been better in the long run. But no one had told him, and he knew, deep down in his heart, that he would not have listened if they had. It had been so easy. Big money—sharp, glorious fights—periods of rest and loafing in between—a following of eager flatterers, the slaps on the back, the shakes of the hand, the toffs glad to buy him a drink for the privilege of five minutes' talk—and the glory of it, the yelling houses, the whirlwind finish, the referee's 'King wins!' and his name in the sporting columns next day.

Those had been times! But he realized now, in his slow, ruminating way, that it was the old uns he had been putting away. He was Youth, rising; and they were Age, sinking. No wonder it had been easy—they with their swollen veins and battered knuckles and weary in the bones of them from the long battles they had already fought. He remembered the time he put out old Stowsher Bill, at Rush-Cutters Bay, in the eighteenth round, and how old Bill had cried afterward in the dressing-room like a baby. Perhaps old Bill's rent had been overdue. Perhaps he'd had at home a missus an' a couple of kiddies. And perhaps Bill, that very day of the fight, had had a hungering for a piece of steak. Bill had fought game and taken incredible punishment. He could see now, after he had gone through the mill himself, that Stowsher Bill had fought for a bigger stake, that night twenty years ago, than had young

Tom King, who had fought for glory and easy money. No wonder Stowsher Bill had cried afterward in the dressing-room.

Well, a man had only so many fights in him, to begin with. It was the iron law of the game. One man might have a hundred hard fights in him, another man only twenty; each, according to the make of him and the quality of his fibre, had a definite number, and, when he had fought them, he was done. Yes, he had had more fights in him than most of them, and he had had far more than his share of the hard, gruelling fights—the kind that worked the heart and lungs to bursting, that took the elastic out of the arteries and made hard knots of muscle out of Youth's sleek suppleness, that wore out nerve and stamina and made brain and bones weary from excess of effort and endurance overwrought. Yes, he had done better than all of them. There was none of his old fighting partners left. He was the last of the old guard. He had seen them all finished, and he had had a hand in finishing some of them.

They had tried him out against the old uns, and one after another he had put them away—laughing when, like old Stowsher Bill, they cried in the dressing-room. And now he was an old un, and they tried out the youngsters on him. There was that bloke, Sandel. He had come over from New Zealand with a record behind him. But nobody in Australia knew anything about him, so they put him up against old Tom King. If Sandel made a showing, he would be given better men to fight, with bigger purses to win; so it was to be depended upon that he would put up a fierce battle. He had everything to win by it—money and glory and career; and Tom King was the grizzled old chopping-block that guarded the highway to fame and fortune. And he had nothing to win except thirty quid, to pay to the landlord and the tradesmen. And, as Tom King thus ruminated, there came to his stolid vision the form of Youth, glorious Youth, rising exultant and invincible, supple of muscle and silken of skin, with heart and lungs that had never been tired and torn and that laughed at limitation of effort. Yes, Youth was the Nemesis. It destroyed the old uns and recked not that, in so doing, it destroyed itself. It enlarged its arteries and smashed its knuckles, and was in turn destroyed by Youth. For Youth was ever youthful. It was only Age that grew old.

At Castlereagh Street he turned to the left, and three blocks along came to the Gaiety. A crowd of young larrikins hanging outside the door made respectful way for him, and he heard one say to another: 'That's 'im! That's Tom King!'

Inside, on the way to his dressing-room, he encountered the secretary, a keen-eyed, shrewd-faced young man, who shook his hand.

'How are you feelin', Tom?' he asked.

'Fit as a fiddle,' King answered, though he knew that he lied, and that if he had a quid, he would give it right there for a good piece of steak.

When he emerged from the dressing-room, his seconds behind him, and came down the aisle to the squared ring in the centre of the hall, a burst of greeting and applause went up from the waiting crowd. He acknowledged salutations right and left, though few of the faces did he know. Most of them were the faces of kiddies unborn when he was winning his first laurels in the squared ring. He leaped lightly to the raised platform and ducked through the ropes to his corner, where he sat down on a folding stool. Jack Ball, the referee, came over and shook his hand. Ball was a broken-down pugilist who for over ten years had not entered the ring as a principal. King was glad that he had him for referee. They were both old uns. If he should rough it with Sandel a bit beyond the rules, he knew Ball could be depended upon to pass it by.

Aspiring young heavyweights, one after another, were climbing into the ring and being presented to the audience by the referee. Also, he issued their challenges for them.

'Young Pronto,' Bill announced, 'from North Sydney, challenges the winner for fifty pounds side bet.'

The audience applauded, and applauded again as Sandel himself sprang through the ropes and sat down in his corner. Tom King looked across the ring at him curiously, for in a few minutes they would be locked together in merciless combat, each trying with all the force of him to knock the other into unconsciousness. But little could he see, for Sandel, like himself, had trousers and sweater on over his ring costume. His face was strongly handsome, crowned with a curly mop of yellow hair, while his thick, muscular neck hinted at bodily magnificence.

Young Pronto went to one corner and then the other, shaking hands with the principals and dropping down out of the ring. The challenges went on. Ever Youth climbed through the ropes—Youth unknown, but insatiable—crying out to mankind that with strength and skill it would match issues with the winner. A few years before, in his own heyday of invincibleness, Tom King would have been amused and bored by these preliminaries. But now he sat fascinated, unable to shake the vision of Youth from his eyes. Always were these youngsters rising up in the boxing game, springing through the ropes and shouting their defiance; and always were the old uns going down before them. They climbed to success over the bodies of the old uns. And ever they came, more and more youngsters—Youth unquenchable and irresistible—and ever they put the old uns away, themselves becoming old uns and travelling the same downward path, while behind them, ever pressing on them, was Youth eternal—the new babies, grown lusty and dragging their elders down, with behind them more babies to the end of time—Youth that must have its will and that will never die.

King glanced over to the press box and nodded to Morgan, of the *Sportsman*, and *Corbett*, of the *Referee*. Then he held out his hands, while Sid Sullivan and Charley Bates, his seconds, slipped on his gloves and laced them tight, closely watched by one of

Sandel's seconds, who first examined critically the tapes on King's knuckles. A second of his own was in Sandel's corner, performing a like office. Sandel's trousers were pulled off, and, as he stood up, his sweater was skinned off over his head. And Tom King, looking, saw Youth incarnate, deep-chested, heavy-thewed, with muscles that slipped and slid like live things under the white satin skin. The whole body was acrawl with life, and Tom King knew that it was a life that had never oozed its freshness out through the aching pores during the long fights wherein Youth paid its toll and departed not quite so young as when it entered.

The two men advanced to meet each other, and, as the gong sounded and the seconds clattered out of the ring with the folding stools, they shook hands and instantly took their fighting attitudes. And instantly, like a mechanism of steel and springs balanced on a hair trigger, Sandel was in and out and in again, landing a left to the eyes, a right to the ribs, ducking a counter, dancing lightly away and dancing menacingly back again. He was swift and clever. It was a dazzling exhibition. The house yelled its approbation. But King was not dazzled. He had fought too many fights and too many youngsters. He knew the blows for what they were—too quick and too deft to be dangerous. Evidently Sandel was going to rush things from the start. It was to be expected. It was the way of Youth, expending its splendour and excellence in wild insurgence and furious onslaught, overwhelming opposition with its own unlimited glory of strength and desire.

Sandel was in and out, here, there, and everywhere, light-footed and eager-hearted, a living wonder of white flesh and stinging muscle that wove itself into a dazzling fabric of attack, slipping and leaping like a flying shuttle from action to action through a thousand actions, all of them centred upon the destruction of Tom King, who stood between him and fortune. And Tom King patiently endured. He knew his business, and he knew Youth now that Youth was no longer his. There was nothing to do till the other lost some of his steam, was his thought, and he grinned to himself as he deliberately ducked so as to receive a heavy blow on the top of his head. It was a wicked thing to do, yet eminently fair according to the rules of the boxing game. A man was supposed to take care of his own knuckles, and, if he insisted on hitting an opponent on the top of the head, he did so at his own peril. King could have ducked lower and let the blow whiz harmlessly past, but he remembered his own early fights and how he smashed his first knuckle on the head of the Welsh Terror. He was but playing the game. That duck had accounted for one of Sandel's knuckles. Not that Sandel would mind it now. He would go on, superbly regardless, hitting as hard as ever throughout the fight. But later on, when the long ring battles had begun to tell, he would regret that knuckle and look back and remember how he smashed it on Tom King's head.

The first round was all Sandel's, and he had the house yelling with the rapidity of his whirlwind rushes. He overwhelmed King with avalanches of punches, and King did nothing. He never struck once, contenting himself with covering up, blocking and ducking and clinching to avoid punishment. He occasionally feinted, shook his head when the weight of a punch landed, and moved stolidly about, never leaping or springing or wasting an ounce of strength. Sandel must foam the froth of Youth away before discreet Age could dare to retaliate. All King's movements were slow and methodical, and his heavy-lidded, slow-moving eyes gave him the appearance of being half asleep or dazed. Yet they were eyes that saw everything, that had been trained to see everything through all his twenty years and odd in the ring. They were eyes that did not blink or waver before an impending blow, but that coolly saw and measured distance.

Seated in his corner for the minute's rest at the end of the round, he lay back with outstretched legs, his arms resting on the right angle of the ropes, his chest and abdomen heaving frankly and deeply as he gulped down the air driven by the towels of his seconds. He listened with closed eyes to the voices of the house, 'Why don't yeh fight, Tom?' many were crying. 'Yeh ain't afraid of 'im, are yeh?'

'Muscle-bound,' he heard a man on a front seat comment. 'He can't move quicker. Two to one on Sandel, in quids.'

The gong struck and the two men advanced from their corners. Sandel came forward fully three-quarters of the distance, eager to begin again; but King was content to advance the shorter distance. It was in line with his policy of economy. He had not been well trained, and he had not had enough to eat, and every step counted. Besides, he had already walked two miles to the ringside. It was a repetition of the first round, with Sandel attacking like a whirlwind and with the audience indignantly demanding why King did not fight. Beyond feinting and several slowly delivered and ineffectual blows he did nothing save block and stall and clinch. Sandel wanted to make the pace fast, while King, out of his wisdom, refused to accommodate him. He grinned with a certain wistful pathos in his ring-battered countenance, and went on cherishing his strength with the jealousy of which only Age is capable. Sandel was Youth, and he threw his strength away with the munificent abandon of Youth. To King belonged the ring generalship, the wisdom bred of long, aching fights. He watched with cool eyes and head, moving slowly and waiting for Sandel's froth to foam away. To the majority of the onlookers it seemed as though King was hopelessly outclassed, and they voiced their opinion in offers of three to one on Sandel. But there were wise ones, a few, who knew King of old time, and who covered what they considered easy money.

The third round began as usual, one-sided, with Sandel doing all the leading and delivering all the punishment. A half-minute had passed when Sandel, overconfident, left an opening. King's eyes and right arm flashed in the same instant. It was his first real blow—a hook, with the twisted arch of the arm to make it rigid, and with all the weight of the half-pivoted body behind it. It was like a sleepy-seeming lion suddenly thrusting out a lightning paw. Sandel, caught on the side of the jaw, was felled like a bullock. The audience gasped and murmured awe-stricken applause. The man was not muscle-bound, after all, and he could drive a blow like a trip-hammer.

Sandel was shaken. He rolled over and attempted to rise, but the sharp yells from his seconds to take the count restrained him. He knelt on one knee, ready to rise, and waited, while the referee stood over him, counting the seconds loudly in his ear. At the ninth he rose in fighting attitude, and Tom King, facing him, knew regret that the blow had not been an inch nearer the point of the jaw. That would have been a knockout, and he could have carried the thirty quid home to the missus and the kiddies.

The round continued to the end of its three minutes, Sandel for the first time respectful of his opponent and King slow of movement and sleepy-eyed as ever. As the round neared its close, King, warned of the fact by sight of the seconds crouching outside ready for the spring in through the ropes, worked the fight around to his own corner. And when the gong struck, he sat down immediately on the waiting stool, while Sandel had to walk all the way across the diagonal of the square to his own corner. It was a little thing, but it was the sum of little things that counted. Sandel was compelled to walk that many more steps, to give up that much energy, and to lose a part of the precious minute of rest. At the beginning of every round King loafed slowly out from his corner, forcing his opponent to advance the greater distance. The end of every round found the fight manoeuvred by King into his own corner so that he could immediately sit down.

Two more rounds went by, in which King was parsimonious of effort and Sandel prodigal. The latter's attempt to force a fast pace made King uncomfortable, for a fair percentage of the multitudinous blows showered upon him went home. Yet King persisted in his dogged slowness, despite the crying of the young hotheads for him to go in and fight. Again, in the sixth round, Sandel was careless, again Tom King's fearful right flashed out to the jaw, and again Sandel took the nine seconds count.

By the seventh round Sandel's pink of condition was gone, and he settled down to what he knew was to be the hardest fight in his experience. Tom King was an old un, but a better old un than he had ever encountered—an old un who never lost his head, who was remarkably able at defence, whose blows had the impact of a knotted club, and who had a knockout in either hand. Nevertheless, Tom King dared not hit often. He never forgot his battered knuckles, and knew that every hit must count if the knuckles were to last out the fight. As he sat in his corner, glancing across at his opponent, the thought came to him that the sum of his wisdom and Sandel's youth would constitute a world's champion heavyweight. But that was the trouble. Sandel would never become a world champion. He lacked the wisdom, and the only way for him to get it was to buy it with Youth; and when wisdom was his, Youth would have been spent in buying it.

King took every advantage he knew. He never missed an opportunity to clinch, and in effecting most of the clinches his shoulder drove stiffly into the other's ribs. In the philosophy of the ring a shoulder was as good as a punch so far as damage was concerned, and a great deal better so far as concerned expenditure of effort. Also, in the clinches King rested his weight on his opponent, and was loath to let go. This compelled the interference of the referee, who tore them apart, always assisted by Sandel, who had not yet learned to rest. He could not refrain from using those glorious flying arms and writhing muscles of his, and when the other rushed into a clinch, striking shoulder against ribs, and with head resting under Sandel's left arm, Sandel almost invariably swung his right behind his own back and into the projecting face. It was a clever stroke, much admired by the audience, but it was not dangerous, and was, therefore, just that much wasted strength. But Sandel was tireless and unaware of limitations, and King grinned and doggedly endured.

Sandel developed a fierce right to the body, which made it appear that King was taking an enormous amount of punishment, and it was only the old ringsters who appreciated the deft touch of King's left glove to the other's biceps just before the impact of the blow. It was true, the blow landed each time; but each time it was robbed of its power by that touch on the biceps. In the ninth round, three times inside a minute, King's right hooked its twisted arch to the jaw; and three times Sandel's body, heavy as it was, was levelled to the mat. Each time he took the nine seconds allowed him and rose to his feet, shaken and jarred, but still strong. He had lost much of his speed, and he wasted less effort. He was fighting grimly; but he continued to draw upon his chief asset, which was Youth. King's chief asset was experience. As his vitality had dimmed and his vigour abated, he had replaced them with cunning, with wisdom born of the long fights and with a careful shepherding of strength. Not alone had he learned never to make a superfluous movement, but he had learned how to seduce an opponent into throwing his strength away. Again and again, by feint of foot and hand and body he continued to inveigle Sandel into leaping back, ducking, or countering. King rested, but he never permitted Sandel to rest. It was the strategy of Age.

Early in the tenth round King began stopping the other's rushes with straight lefts to the face, and Sandel, grown wary, responded by drawing the left, then by ducking it and delivering his right in a swinging hook to the side of the head. It was too high up to be vitally effective; but when first it landed, King knew the old, familiar descent of the black veil of unconsciousness across his mind. For the instant, or for the slightest fraction of an instant, rather, he ceased. In the one moment he saw his opponent ducking out of his field of vision and the background of white, watching faces; in the next moment he again saw his opponent and the background of faces. It was as if he had slept for a time and just opened his eyes again, and yet the interval of unconsciousness was so microscopically short that there had been no time for him to fall. The audience saw him totter and his knees give, and then saw him recover and tuck his chin deeper into the shelter of his left shoulder.

Several times Sandel repeated the blow, keeping King partially dazed, and then the latter worked out his defence, which was also a counter. Feinting with his left he took a half-step backward, at the same time upper cutting with the whole strength of his right. So accurately was it timed that it landed squarely on Sandel's face in the full, downward sweep of the duck, and Sandel lifted in the air and curled backward, striking the mat on his head and shoulders. Twice King achieved this, then turned loose and hammered his opponent to the ropes. He gave Sandel no chance to rest or to set himself, but smashed blow in upon blow till the house rose to its feet and the air was filled with an unbroken roar of applause. But Sandel's strength and endurance were superb, and he continued to stay on his feet. A knockout seemed certain, and a captain of police, appalled at the dreadful punishment, arose by the ringside to stop the fight. The gong struck for the end of the round and Sandel staggered to his corner, protesting to the captain that he was sound and strong. To prove it, he threw two back air-springs, and the police captain gave in.

Tom King, leaning back in his corner and breathing hard, was disappointed. If the fight had been stopped, the referee, perforce, would have rendered him the decision and the purse would have been his. Unlike Sandel, he was not fighting for glory or career, but for thirty quid. And now Sandel would recuperate in the minute of rest.

Youth will be served—this saying flashed into King's mind,

and he remembered the first time he had heard it, the night when he had put away Stowsher Bill. The toff who had bought him a drink after the fight and patted him on the shoulder had used those words. Youth will be served! The toff was right. And on that night in the long ago he had been Youth. Tonight Youth sat in the opposite corner. As for himself, he had been fighting for half an hour now, and he was an old man. Had he fought like Sandel, he would not have lasted fifteen minutes. But the point was that he did not recuperate. Those upstanding arteries and that sorely tried heart would not enable him to gather strength in the intervals between the rounds. And he had not had sufficient strength in him to begin with. His legs were heavy under him and beginning to cramp. He should not have walked those two miles to the fight. And there was the steak which he had got up longing for that morning. A great and terrible hatred rose up in him for the butchers who had refused him credit. It was hard for an old man to go into a fight without enough to eat. And a piece of steak was such a little thing, a few pennies at best; yet it meant thirty quid to him.

With the gong that opened the eleventh round, Sandel rushed, making a show of freshness which he did not really possess. King knew it for what it was—a bluff as old as the game itself. He clinched to save himself, then, going free, allowed Sandel to get set. This was what King desired. He feinted with his left, drew the answering duck and swinging upward hook, then made the half-step backward, delivered the upper cut full to the face and crumpled Sandel over to the mat. After that he never let him rest, receiving punishment himself, but inflicting far more, smashing Sandel to the ropes, hooking and driving all manner of blows into him, tearing away from his clinches or punching him out of attempted clinches, and ever when Sandel would have fallen, catching him with one uplifting hand and with the other immediately smashing him into the ropes where he could not fall.

The house by this time had gone mad, and it was his house, nearly every voice yelling: 'Go it, Tom!' 'Get 'im! Get 'im!' 'You've got 'im, Tom! You've got 'im!' It was to be a whirlwind finish, and that was what a ringside audience paid to see.

And Tom King, who for half an hour had conserved his strength, now expended it prodigally in the one great effort he knew he had in him. It was his one chance—now or not at all. His strength was waning fast, and his hope was that before the last of it ebbed out of him he would have beaten his opponent down for the count. And as he continued to strike and force, coolly estimating the weight of his blows and the quality of the damage wrought, he realized how hard a man Sandel was to knock out. Stamina and endurance were his to an extreme degree, and they were the virgin stamina and endurance of Youth. Sandel was certainly a coming man. He had it in him. Only out of such rugged fibre were successful fighters fashioned.

Sandel was reeling and staggering, but Tom King's legs were cramping and his knuckles going back on him. Yet he steeled himself to strike the fierce blows, every one of which brought anguish to his tortured hands. Though now he was receiving practically no punishment, he was weakening as rapidly as the other. His blows went home, but there was no longer the weight behind them, and each blow was the result of a severe effort of will. His legs were like lead, and they dragged visibly under him; while Sandel's backers, cheered by this symptom, began calling encouragement to their man.

King was spurred to a burst of effort. He delivered two blows in succession—a left, a trifle too high, to the solar plexus, and a right cross to the jaw. They were not heavy blows, yet so weak and dazed was Sandel that he went down and lay quivering. The referee stood over him, shouting the count of the fatal seconds in his ear. If before the tenth second was called, he did not rise, the fight was lost. The house stood in hushed silence. King rested on trembling legs. A mortal dizziness was upon him, and before his eyes the sea of faces sagged and swayed, while to his ears, as from a remote distance, came the count of the referee. Yet he looked upon the fight as his. It was impossible that a man so punished could rise.

Only Youth could rise, and Sandel rose. At the fourth second he rolled over on his face and groped blindly for the ropes. By the seventh second he had dragged himself to his knee, where he rested, his head rolling groggily on his shoulders. As the referee cried 'Nine!' Sandel stood upright, in proper stalling position, his left arm wrapped about his face, his right wrapped about his stomach. Thus were his vital points guarded, while he lurched forward toward King in the hope of effecting a clinch and gaining more time.

At the instant Sandel arose, King was at him, but the two blows he delivered were muffled on the stalled arms. The next moment Sandel was in the clinch and holding on desperately while the referee strove to drag the two men apart. King helped to force himself free. He knew the rapidity with which Youth recovered, and he knew that Sandel was his if he could prevent that recovery. One stiff punch would do it. Sandel was his, indubitably his. He had outgeneralled him, outfought him, outpointed him. Sandel reeled out of the clinch, balanced on the hair line between defeat or survival. One good blow would topple him over and down and out. And Tom King, in a flash of bitterness, remembered the piece of steak and wished that he had it then behind that necessary punch he must deliver. He nerved himself for the blow, but it was not heavy enough nor swift enough. Sandel swayed, but did not fall, staggering back to the ropes and holding on. King staggered after him, and, with a pang like that of dissolution, delivered another blow. But his body had deserted him. All that was left of him was a fighting intelligence that was dimmed and clouded from exhaustion. The blow that was aimed for the jaw struck no higher than the shoulder. He had willed the blow higher, but the tired muscles had not been able to obey. And, from the impact of the blow, Tom King himself reeled back and nearly fell. Once again he strove. This time his punch missed altogether, and, from absolute weakness, he fell against Sandel and clinched, holding on to him to save himself from sinking to the floor.

King did not attempt to free himself. He had shot his bolt. He was gone. And Youth had been served. Even in the clinch he could feel Sandel growing stronger against him. When the referee thrust them apart, there, before his eyes, he saw Youth recuperate. From instant to instant Sandel grew stronger. His punches, weak and futile at first, became stiff and accurate. Tom King's bleared eyes saw the gloved fist driving at his jaw, and he willed to guard it by interposing his arm. He saw the danger, willed the act; but the arm was too heavy. It seemed burdened with a hundredweight of lead. It would not lift itself, and he strove to lift it with his soul. Then the gloved fist landed home. He experienced a sharp snap that was like an electric spark, and, simultaneously, the veil of blackness enveloped him.

When he opened his eyes again he was in his corner, and he heard the yelling of the audience like the roar of the surf at Bondi Beach. A wet sponge was being pressed against the base of his brain, and Sid Sullivan was blowing cold water in a refreshing spray over his face and chest. His gloves had already been removed, and Sandel, bending over him, was shaking his hand. He bore no ill-will toward the man who had put him out, and he returned the grip with a heartiness that made his battered knuckles protest. Then Sandel stepped to the centre of the ring and the audience hushed its pandemonium to hear him accept young Pronto's challenge and offer to increase the side bet to one hundred pounds. King looked on apathetically while his seconds mopped the streaming water from him, dried his face, and prepared him to leave the ring. He felt hungry. It was not the ordinary, gnawing kind, but a great faintness, a palpitation at the pit of the stomach that communicated itself to all his body. He remembered back into the fight to the moment when he had Sandel swaying and tottering on the hair-line balance of defeat. Ah, that piece of steak would have done it! He had lacked just that for the decisive blow, and he had lost. It was all because of the piece of steak.

His seconds were half-supporting him as they helped him through the ropes. He tore free from them, ducked through the ropes unaided, and leaped heavily to the floor, following on their heels as they forced a passage for him down the crowded centre aisle. Leaving the dressing-room for the street, in the entrance to the hall, some young fellow spoke to him.

'W'y didn't yuh go in an' get 'im when yuh 'ad 'im?' the young fellow asked.

'Aw, go to hell!' said Tom King, and passed down the steps to the sidewalk.

The doors of the public house at the corner were swinging wide, and he saw the lights and the smiling barmaids, heard the many voices discussing the fight and the prosperous chink of money on the bar. Somebody called to him to have a drink. He hesitated perceptibly, then refused and went on his way.

He had not a copper in his pocket, and the two-mile walk home seemed very long. He was certainly getting old. Crossing the Domain, he sat down suddenly on a bench, unnerved by the thought of the missus sitting up for him, waiting to learn the outcome of the fight. That was harder than any knockout, and it seemed almost impossible to face.

He felt weak and sore, and the pain of his smashed knuckles warned him that, even if he could find a job at navvy work, it would be a week before he could grip a pick handle or a shovel. The hunger palpitation at the pit of the stomach was sickening. His wretchedness overwhelmed him, and into his eyes came an unwonted moisture. He covered his face with his hands, and, as he cried, he remembered Stowsher Bill and how he had served him that night in the long ago. Poor old Stowsher Bill! He could understand now why Bill had cried in the dressing-room.

2

BROWN WOLF

She had delayed, because of the dew-wet grass, in order to put on her overshoes, and when she emerged from the house found her waiting husband absorbed in the wonder of a bursting almond-bud. She sent a questing glance across the tall grass and in and out among the orchard trees.

'Where's Wolf?' she asked.

'He was here a moment ago.' Walt Irvine drew himself away with a jerk from the metaphysics and poetry of the organic miracle of blossom, and surveyed the landscape.

'He was running a rabbit the last I saw of him.'

'Wolf! Wolf! Here Wolf!' she called, as they left the clearing and took the trail that led down through the waxen-belled manzanita jungle to the county road.

Irvine thrust between his lips the little finger of each hand and lent to her efforts a shrill whistling.

She covered her ears hastily and made a wry grimace.

'My! for a poet, delicately attuned and all the rest of it, you can make unlovely noises. My ear drums are pierced. You outwhistle—'

'Orpheus.'

'I was about to say a street-arab,' she concluded severely.

'Poesy does not prevent one from being practical—at least it doesn't prevent *me*. Mine is no futility of genius that can't sell gems to the magazines.'

He assumed a mock extravagance, and went on:

'I am no attic singer, no ballroom warbler. And why? Because I am practical. Mine is no squalor of song that cannot transmute itself, with proper exchange value, into a flower-crowned cottage, a sweet mountain meadow, a grove of redwoods, an orchard of thirty-seven trees, one long row of blackberries and two short rows of strawberries, to say nothing of a quarter of a mile of gurgling brook. I am a beauty merchant, a trader in song, and I pursue utility, dear Madge. I sing a song, and thanks to the magazine editors I transmute my song into a waft of the west wind sighing through our redwoods, into a murmur of waters over mossy stones that sings back to me another song than the one I sang and yet the same song wonderfully—er—transmuted.'

'O that all your song-transmutations were as successful!' she laughed.

'Name one that wasn't.'

'Those two beautiful sonnets that you transmuted into the cow that was accounted the worst milker in the township.'

'She was beautiful—' he began,

'But she didn't give milk,' Madge interrupted.

'But she *was* beautiful, now, wasn't she?' he insisted.

'And here's where beauty and utility fall out,' was her reply. 'And there's the Wolf!'

From the thicket-covered hillside came a crashing of underbrush, and then, forty feet above them, on the edge of the sheer wall of rock, appeared a wolf's head and shoulders. His braced forepaws dislodged a pebble, and with sharp-pricked ears and peering eyes he watched the fall of the pebble till it struck at their feet. Then he transferred his gaze and with open mouth laughed down at them.

'You Wolf, you!' and 'You blessed Wolf!' the man and woman

called out to him.

The ears flattened back and down at the sound, and the head seemed to snuggle under the caress of an invisible hand.

They watched him scramble backward into the thicket, then proceeded on their way. Several minutes later, rounding a turn in the trail where the descent was less precipitous, he joined them in the midst of a miniature avalanche of pebbles and loose soil. He was not demonstrative. A pat and a rub around the ears from the man, and a more prolonged caressing from the woman, and he was away down the trail in front of them, gliding effortlessly over the ground in true wolf fashion.

In build and coat and brush he was a huge timber-wolf; but the lie was given to his wolfhood by his colour and marking. There the dog unmistakably advertised itself. No wolf was ever coloured like him. He was brown, deep brown, red-brown, an orgy of browns. Back and shoulders were a warm brown that paled on the sides and underneath to a yellow that was dingy because of the brown that lingered in it. The white of the throat and paws and the spots over the eyes was dirty because of the persistent and ineradicable brown, while the eyes themselves were twin topazes, golden and brown.

The man and woman loved the dog very much; perhaps this was because it had been such a task to win his love. It had been no easy matter when he first drifted in mysteriously out of nowhere to their little mountain cottage. Footsore and famished, he had killed a rabbit under their very noses and under their very windows, and then crawled away and slept by the spring at the foot of the blackberry bushes. When Walt Irvine went down to inspect the intruder, he was snarled at for his pains, and Madge likewise was snarled at when she went down to present, as a peace offering, a large pan of bread and milk.

A most unsociable dog he proved to be, resenting all their advances, refusing to let them lay hands on him, menacing them with bared fangs and bristling hair. Nevertheless he remained, sleeping and resting by the spring, and eating the food they gave him after they set it down at a safe distance and retreated. His wretched physical condition explained why he lingered; and when he had recuperated, after several days' sojourn, he disappeared.

And this would have been the end of him, so far as Irvine and his wife were concerned, had not Irvine at that particular time been called away into the northern part of the state. Riding along on the train, near to the line between California and Oregon, he chanced to look out of the window and saw his unsociable guest sliding along the wagon road, brown and wolfish, tired yet tireless, dust-covered and soiled with two hundred miles of travel.

Now Irvine was a man of impulse, a poet. He got off the train at the next station, bought a piece of meat at a butcher shop, and captured the vagrant on the outskirts of the town. The return trip was made in the baggage car, and so Wolf came a second time to the mountain cottage. Here he was tied up for a week and made love to by the man and woman. But it was very circumspect love-making. Remote and alien as a traveller from another planet, he snarled down their soft-spoken love-words. He never barked. In all the time they had him he was never known to bark.

To win him became a problem. Irvine liked problems. He had a metal plate made, on which was stamped: Return to Walt Irvine, Glen Ellen, Sonoma County, California. This was riveted to a collar and strapped about the dog's neck. Then he was turned loose, and promptly he disappeared. A day later came a telegram from Mendocino County. In twenty hours he had made over a hundred miles to the north, and was still going when captured.

He came back by Wells Fargo Express, was tied up three days, and was loosed on the fourth and lost. This time he gained southern Oregon before he was caught and returned. Always, as soon as he received his liberty, he fled away, and always he fled north. He was possessed of an obsession that drove him north.

The homing instinct, Irvine called it, after he had expended the selling price of a sonnet in getting the animal back from northern Oregon.

Another time the brown wanderer succeeded in traversing half the length of California, all of Oregon, and most of Washington, before he was picked up and returned 'Collect'. A remarkable thing was the speed with which he travelled. Fed up and rested, as soon as he was loosed he devoted all his energy to getting over the ground. On the first day's run he was known to cover as high as a hundred and fifty miles, and after that he would average a hundred miles a day until caught. He always arrived back lean and hungry and savage, and always departed fresh and vigorous, cleaving his way northward in response to some prompting of his being that no one could understand.

But at last, after a futile year of flight, he accepted the inevitable and elected to remain at the cottage where first he had killed the rabbit and slept by the spring. Even after that, a long time elapsed before the man and woman succeeded in patting him. It was a great victory, for they alone were allowed to put hands on him. He was fastidiously exclusive, and no guest at the cottage ever succeeded in making up to him. A low growl greeted such approach; if anyone had the hardihood to come nearer, the lips lifted, the naked fangs appeared, and the growl became a snarl—a snarl so terrible and malignant that it awed the stoutest of them, as it likewise awed the farmers' dogs that knew ordinary dog-snarling, but had never seen wolf-snarling before.

He was without antecedents. His history began with Walt and Madge. He had come up from the south, but never a clue did they get of the owner from whom he had evidently fled. Mrs Johnson, their nearest neighbour and the one who supplied them with milk, proclaimed him a Klondike dog. Her brother was burrowing for frozen pay-streaks in that far country, and so she constituted herself an authority on the subject.

But they did not dispute her. There were the tips of Wolf's ears, obviously so severely frozen at some time that they would never quite heal again. Besides, he looked like the photographs of the Alaskan dogs they saw published in magazines and newspapers. They often speculated over his past, and tried to conjure up (from what they had read and heard) what his Northland life had been. That the Northland still drew him, they knew; for at night they sometimes heard him crying softly; and when the north wind blew and the bite of frost was in the air, a great restlessness would come upon him and he would lift a mournful lament which they knew to be the long wolf-howl. Yet he never barked. No provocation was great enough to draw from him that canine cry.

Long discussion they had, during the time of winning him, as to whose dog he was. Each claimed him, and each proclaimed loudly any expression of affection made by him. But the man had the better of it at first, chiefly because he was a man. It was patent that Wolf had had no experience with women. He did not understand women. Madge's skirts were something he never quite accepted. The swish of them was enough to set him a-bristle with suspicion, and on a windy day she could not approach him at all.

On the other hand, it was Madge who fed him; also it was she who ruled the kitchen, and it was by her favour, and her favour alone, that he was permitted to come within that sacred precinct. It was because of these things that she bade fair to overcome the handicap of her garments. Then it was that Walt put forth special effort, making it a practice to have Wolf lie at his feet while he wrote, and, between petting and talking, losing much time from his work. Walt won in the end, and his victory was most probably due to the fact that he was a man, though Madge averred that they would have had another quarter of a mile of gurgling brook, and at least two west winds sighing through their redwoods, had Walt properly devoted his energies to song-transmutation and left Wolf alone to exercise a natural taste and an unbiased judgment.

'It's about time I heard from those triolets,' Walt said, after a silence of five minutes, during which they had swung steadily down the trail. 'There'll be a cheque at the post office, I know, and we'll transmute it into beautiful buckwheat flour, a gallon of maple syrup, and a new pair of overshoes for you.'

'And into beautiful milk from Mrs Johnson's beautiful cow,' Madge added. 'Tomorrow's the first of the month, you know.'

Walt scowled unconsciously; then his face brightened, and he clapped his hand to his breast pocket.

'Never mind. I have here a nice beautiful new cow, the best milker in California.'

'When did you write it?' she demanded eagerly. Then, reproachfully, 'And you never showed it to me.'

'I saved it to read to you on the way to the post office, in a spot remarkably like this one,' he answered, indicating, with a wave of his hand, a dry log on which to sit.

A tiny stream flowed out of a dense fern-brake, slipped down a mossy-lipped stone, and ran across the path at their feet. From the valley arose the mellow song of meadow-larks, while about them, in and out, through sunshine and shadow, fluttered great yellow butterflies.

Up from below came another sound that broke in upon Walt reading softly from his manuscript. It was a crunching of heavy feet, punctuated now and again by the clattering of a displaced stone. As Walt finished and looked to his wife for approval, a man came into view around the turn of the trail. He was bare-headed and sweaty. With a handkerchief in one hand he mopped his face, while in the other hand he carried a new hat and a wilted starched collar which he had removed from his neck. He was a well-built man, and his muscles seemed on the point of bursting out of the painfully new and ready-made black clothes he wore.

'Warm day,' Walt greeted him. Walt believed in country democracy, and never missed an opportunity to practise it.

The man paused and nodded.

'I guess I ain't used much to the warm,' he vouchsafed half apologetically. 'I'm more accustomed to zero weather.'

'You don't find any of that in this country,' Walt laughed.

'Should say not,' the man answered. 'An' I ain't here a-lookin' for it neither. I'm tryin' to find my sister. Mebbe you know where she lives. Her name's Johnson, Mrs William Johnson.'

'You're not her Klondike brother!' Madge cried, her eyes bright with interest, 'about whom we've heard so much?'

'Yes'm, that's me,' he answered modestly. 'My name's Miller, Skiff Miller. I just thought I'd s'prise her.'

'You are on the right track then. Only you've come by the foot path.' Madge stood up to direct him, pointing up the canyon a quarter of a mile. 'You see that blasted redwood? Take the little trail turning off to the right. It's the short cut to her house. You can't miss it.'

'Yes'm, thank you, ma'am,' he said. He made tentative efforts to go, but seemed awkwardly rooted to the spot. He was gazing at her with an open admiration of which he was quite unconscious, and which was drowning, along with him, in the rising sea of embarrassment in which he floundered.

'We'd like to hear you tell about the Klondike,' Madge said. 'Mayn't we come over some day while you are at your sister's? Or, better yet, won't you come over and have dinner with us?'

'Yes'm, thank you, ma'am,' he mumbled mechanically. Then he caught himself up and added: 'I ain't stoppin' long. I got to be pullin' north again. I go out on tonight's train. You see, I've got a mail contract with the government.'

When Madge had said that it was too bad, he made another futile effort to go. But he could not take his eyes from her face. He forgot his embarrassment in his admiration, and it was her turn to flush and feel uncomfortable.

It was at this juncture, when Walt had just decided it was time for him to be saying something to relieve the strain, that Wolf, who had been away nosing through the brush, trotted wolf-like into view.

Skiff Miller's abstraction disappeared. The pretty woman before him passed out of his field of vision. He had eyes only for the dog, and a great wonder came into his face.

'Well, I'll be damned!' he enunciated slowly and solemnly.

He sat down ponderingly on the log, leaving Madge standing. At the sound of his voice, Wolf's ears had flattened down, then his mouth had opened in a laugh. He trotted slowly up to the stranger and first smelled his hands, then licked them with his tongue.

Skiff Miller patted the dog's head, and slowly and solemnly repeated, 'Well, I'll be damned!'

'Excuse me, ma'am,' he said the next moment. 'I was just s'prised some, that was all.'

'We're surprised, too,' she answered lightly. 'We never saw Wolf make up to a stranger before.'

'Is that what you call him—Wolf?' the man asked.

Madge nodded. 'But I can't understand his friendliness toward you—unless it's because you're from the Klondike. He's a Klondike dog, you know.'

'Yes'm,' Miller said absently. He lifted one of Wolf's forelegs and examined the footpads, pressing them and denting them with his thumb. 'Kind of soft,' he remarked. 'He ain't been on trail for a long time.'

'I say,' Walt broke in, 'it is remarkable the way he lets you handle him.'

Skiff Miller arose, no longer awkward with admiration of Madge, and in a sharp, businesslike manner asked, 'How long have you had him?'

But just then the dog, squirming and rubbing against the newcomer's legs, opened his mouth and barked. It was an explosive bark, brief and joyous, but a bark.

'That's a new one on me,' Skiff Miller remarked.

Walt and Madge stared at each other. The miracle had happened. Wolf had barked.

'It's the first time he ever barked,' Madge said.

'First time I ever heard him, too,' Miller volunteered.

Madge smiled at him. The man was evidently a humorist.

'Of course,' she said, 'since you have only seen him for five minutes.'

Skiff Miller looked at her sharply, seeking in her face the guile her words had led him to suspect.

'I thought you understood,' he said slowly. 'I thought you'd tumbled to it from his makin' up to me. He's my dog. His name ain't Wolf. It's Brown.'

'Oh, Walt!' was Madge's instinctive cry to her husband.

Walt was on the defensive at once.

'How do you know he's your dog?' he demanded.

'Because he is,' was the reply.

'Mere assertion,' Walt said sharply.

In his slow and pondering way, Skiff Miller looked at him, then asked, with a nod of his head toward Madge:

'How d'you know she's your wife? You just say, "Because she is," and I'll say it's mere assertion. The dog's mine. I bred 'm an' raised 'm, an' I guess I ought to know. Look here. I'll prove it to you.'

Skiff Miller turned to the dog. 'Brown!' His voice rang out sharply, and at the sound the dog's ears flattened down as to a caress. 'Gee!' The dog made a swinging turn to the right. 'Now mush-on!' And the dog ceased his swing abruptly and started straight ahead, halting obediently at command.

'I can do it with whistles,' Skiff Miller said proudly. 'He was my lead dog.'

'But you are not going to take him away with you?' Madge asked tremulously.

The man nodded.

'Back into that awful Klondike world of suffering?'

He nodded and added: 'Oh, it ain't so bad as all that. Look at me. Pretty healthy specimen, ain't I?'

'But the dogs! The terrible hardship, the heart-breaking toil, the starvation, the frost! Oh, I've read about it and I know.'

'I nearly ate him once, over on Little Fish River,' Miller volunteered grimly. 'If I hadn't got a moose that day was all that saved 'm.'

'I'd have died first!' Madge cried.

'Things is different down here,' Miller explained. 'You don't have to eat dogs. You think different just about the time you're all in. You've never ben all in, so you don't know anything about it.'

'That's the very point,' she argued warmly. 'Dogs are not eaten in California. Why not leave him here? He is happy. He'll never want for food—you know that. He'll never suffer from cold and hardship. Here all is softness and gentleness. Neither the human nor nature is savage. He will never know a whiplash again. And as for the weather—why, it never snows here.'

'But it's all-fired hot in summer, beggin' your pardon,' Skiff Miller laughed.

'But you do not answer,' Madge continued passionately. 'What have you to offer him in that Northland life?'

'Grub, when I've got it, and that's most of the time,' came the answer.

'And the rest of the time?'

'No grub.'

'And the work?'

'Yes, plenty of work,' Miller blurted out impatiently. 'Work without end, an' famine, an' frost, an all the rest of the miseries—that's what he'll get when he comes with me. But he likes it. He is used to it. He knows that life. He was born to it an' brought up to it. An' you don't know anything about it. You don't know what you're talking about. That's where the dog belongs, and that's where he'll be happiest.'

'The dog doesn't go,' Walt announced in a determined voice. 'So there is no need of further discussion.'

'What's that?' Skiff Miller demanded, his brows lowering and an obstinate flush of blood reddening his forehead.

'I said the dog doesn't go, and that settles it. I don't believe he's your dog. You may have seen him sometime. You may even sometime have driven him for his owner. But his obeying the ordinary driving commands of the Alaskan trail is no demonstration that he is yours. Any dog in Alaska would obey you as he obeyed. Besides, he is undoubtedly a valuable dog, as dogs go in Alaska, and that is sufficient explanation of your desire to get possession of him. Anyway, you've got to prove property.'

Skiff Miller, cool and collected, the obstinate flush a trifle deeper on his forehead, his huge muscles bulging under the black cloth of his coat, carefully looked the poet up and down as though measuring the strength of his slenderness.

The Klondiker's face took on a contemptuous expression as he said finally, 'I reckon there's nothin' in sight to prevent me takin' the dog right here an' now.'

Walt's face reddened, and the striking muscles of his arms and shoulders seemed to stiffen and grow tense. His wife fluttered apprehensively into the breach.

'Maybe Mr Miller is right,' she said. 'I am afraid that he is. Wolf does seem to know him, and certainly he answers to the name of "Brown". He made friends with him instantly, and you know that's something he never did with anybody before. Besides, look at the way he barked. He was just bursting with joy. Joy over what? Without doubt at finding Mr Miller.'

Walt's striking-muscles relaxed, and his shoulders seemed to droop with hopelessness.

'I guess you're right, Madge,' he said. 'Wolf isn't Wolf, but

Brown, and he must belong to Mr Miller.'

'Perhaps Mr Miller will sell him,' she suggested. 'We can buy him.'

Skiff Miller shook his head, no longer belligerent, but kindly, quick to be generous in response to generousness.

'I had five dogs,' he said, casting about for the easiest way to temper his refusal. 'He was the leader. They was the crack team of Alaska. Nothin' could touch 'em. In 1898, I refused five thousand dollars for the bunch. Dogs was high, then, anyway; but that wasn't what made the fancy price. It was the team itself. Brown was the best in the team. That winter I refused twelve hundred for 'm. I didn't sell 'm then, an' I ain't a-sellin' 'm now. Besides, I think a mighty lot of that dog. I've ben lookin' for 'm for three years. It made me fair sick when I found he'd ben stole—not the value of him, but the—well, I liked 'm like hell, that's all, beggin' your pardon. I couldn't believe my eyes when I seen 'm just now. I thought I was dreamin'. It was too good to be true. Why, I was his wet-nurse. I put 'm to bed, snug every night. His mother died, and I brought 'm up on condensed milk at two dollars a can when I couldn't afford it in my own coffee. He never knew any mother but me. He used to suck my finger regular, the darn little cuss—that finger right there!'

And Skiff Miller, too overwrought for speech, held up a forefinger for them to see.

'That very finger,' he managed to articulate, as though it somehow clinched the proof of ownership and the bond of affection.

He was still gazing at his extended finger when Madge began to speak.

'But the dog,' she said. 'You haven't considered the dog.'

Skiff Miller looked puzzled.

'Have you thought about him?' she asked.

'Don't know what you're drivin' at,' was the response.

'Maybe the dog has some choice in the matter,' Madge went on. 'Maybe he has his likes and desires. You have not considered him. You give him no choice. It has never entered your mind that possibly he might prefer California to Alaska. You consider only what you like. You do with him as you would with a sack of potatoes or a bale of hay.'

This was a new way of looking at it, and Miller was visibly impressed as he debated it in his mind. Madge took advantage of his indecision.

'If you really love him, what would be happiness to him would be your happiness also,' she urged.

Skiff Miller continued to debate with himself, and Madge stole a glance of exultation to her husband, who looked back warm approval.

'What do you think?' the Klondiker suddenly demanded.

It was her turn to be puzzled. 'What do you mean?' she asked.

'D'ye think he'd sooner stay in California?'

She nodded her head with positiveness. 'I am sure of it.'

Skiff Miller again debated with himself, though this time aloud, at the same time running his gaze in a judicial way over the mooted animal.

'He was a good worker. He's done a heap of work for me. He never loafed on me, an' he was a joe-dandy at hammerin' a raw team into shape. He's got a head on him. He can do everything but talk. He knows what you say to him. Look at 'm now. He knows we're talkin' about him.'

The dog was lying at Skiff Miller's feet, head close down on paws, ears erect and listening, and eyes that were quick and eager to follow the sound of speech as it fell from the lips of first one and then the other.

'An' there's a lot of work in 'm yet. He's good for years to come. An' I do like him. I like him like hell.'

Once or twice after that Skiff Miller opened his mouth and

closed it again without speaking. Finally he said:

'I'll tell you what I'll do. Your remarks, ma'am, has some weight in them. The dog's worked hard, and maybe he's earned a soft berth an' has got a right to choose. Anyway, we'll leave it up to him. Whatever he says, goes. You people stay right here settin' down. I'll say goodbye and walk off casual-like. If he wants to stay, he can stay. If he wants to come with me, let 'm come. I won't call 'm to come an' don't you call 'm to come back.'

He looked with sudden suspicion at Madge, and added, 'Only you must play fair. No persuadin' after my back is turned.'

'We'll play fair,' Madge began, but Skiff Miller broke in on her assurances.

'I know the ways of women,' he announced. 'Their hearts is soft. When their hearts is touched they're likely to stack the cards, look at the bottom of the deck, an' lie like the devil—beggin' your pardon, ma'am. I'm only discoursin' about women in general.'

'I don't know how to thank you,' Madge quavered.

'I don't see as you've got any call to thank me,' he replied. 'Brown ain't decided yet. Now you won't mind if I go away slow? It's no more'n fair, seein' I'll be out of sight inside a hundred yards.'

Madge agreed, and added, 'And I promise you faithfully that we won't do anything to influence him.'

'Well, then, I might as well be gettin' along,' Skiff Miller said in the ordinary tones of one departing.

At this change in his voice, Wolf lifted his head quickly, and still more quickly got to his feet when the man and woman shook hands. He sprang up on his hind legs, resting his forepaws on her hip and at the same time licking Skiff Miller's hand. When the latter shook hands with Walt, Wolf repeated his act, resting his weight on Walt and licking both men's hands.

'It ain't no picnic, I can tell you that,' were the Klondiker's last words, as he turned and went slowly up the trail.

For the distance of twenty feet Wolf watched him go, himself all eagerness and expectancy, as though waiting for the man to turn and retrace his steps. Then, with a quick low whine, Wolf sprang after him, overtook him, caught his hand between his teeth with reluctant tenderness, and strove gently to make him pause.

Failing in this, Wolf raced back to where Walt Irvine sat, catching his coat sleeve in his teeth and trying vainly to drag him after the retreating man.

Wolf's perturbation began to wax. He desired ubiquity. He wanted to be in two places at the same time, with the old master and the new, and steadily the distance between them was increasing. He sprang about excitedly, making short nervous leaps and twists, now toward one, now toward the other, in painful indecision, not knowing his own mind, desiring both and unable to choose, uttering quick sharp whines and beginning to pant.

He sat down abruptly on his haunches, thrusting his nose upward, the mouth opening and closing with jerking movements, each time opening wider. These jerking movements were in unison with the recurrent spasms that attacked the throat, each spasm severer and more intense than the preceding one. And in accord with jerks and spasms the larynx began to vibrate, at first silently, accompanied by the rush of air expelled from the lungs, then sounding a low, deep note, the lowest in the register of the human ear. All this was the nervous and muscular preliminary to howling.

But just as the howl was on the verge of bursting from the full throat, the wide-opened mouth was closed, the paroxysms ceased, and he looked long and steadily at the retreating man. Suddenly Wolf turned his head, and over his shoulder just as steadily regarded Walt. The appeal was unanswered. Not a word nor a sign did the dog receive, no suggestion and no clue as to what his conduct should be.

A glance ahead to where the old master was nearing the curve of the trail excited him again. He sprang to his feet with a whine, and then, struck by a new idea, turned his attention to Madge. Hitherto he had ignored her, but now, both masters failing him, she alone was left. He went over to her and snuggled his head in her lap, nudging her arm with his nose—an old trick of his when begging for favours. He backed away from her and began writhing and twisting playfully, curvetting and prancing, half rearing and striking his forepaws to the earth, struggling with all his body, from the wheedling eyes and flattening ears to the wagging tail, to express the thought that was in him and that was denied him utterance.

This, too, he soon abandoned. He was depressed by the coldness of these humans who had never been cold before. No response could he draw from them, no help could he get. They did not consider him. They were as dead.

He turned and silently gazed after the old master. Skiff Miller was rounding the curve. In a moment he would be gone from view. Yet he never turned his head, plodding straight onward, slowly and methodically, as though possessed of no interest in what was occurring behind his back.

And in this fashion he went out of view. Wolf waited for him to reappear. He waited a long minute, silently, quietly, without movement, as though turned to stone—withal stone quick with eagerness and desire. He barked once, and waited. Then he turned and trotted back to Walt Irvine. He sniffed his hand and dropped down heavily at his feet, watching the trail where it curved emptily from view.

The tiny stream slipping down the mossy-lipped stone seemed suddenly to increase the volume of its gurgling noise. Save for the meadow-larks, there was no other sound. The great yellow butterflies drifted silently through the sunshine and lost themselves in the drowsy shadows. Madge gazed triumphantly at her husband.

A few minutes later Wolf got upon his feet. Decision and

deliberation marked his movements. He did not glance at the man and woman. His eyes were fixed up the trail. He had made up his mind. They knew it. And they knew, so far as they were concerned, that the ordeal had just begun.

He broke into a trot, and Madge's lips pursed, forming an avenue for the caressing sound that it was the will of her to send forth. But the caressing sound was not made. She was impelled to look at her husband, and she saw the sternness with which he watched her. The pursed lips relaxed, and she sighed inaudibly.

Wolf's trot broke into a run. Wider and wider were the leaps he made. Not once did he turn his head, his wolf's brush standing out straight behind him. He cut sharply across the curve of the trail and was gone.

3

FLUSH OF GOLD

Lon Mcfane was a bit grumpy, what of losing his tobacco pouch, or else he might have told me, before we got to it, something about the cabin at Surprise Lake. All day, turn and turn about, we had spelled each other at going to the fore and breaking trail for the dogs. It was heavy snowshoe work, and did not tend to make a man voluble, yet Lon McFane might have found breath enough at noon, when we stopped to boil coffee, with which to tell me. But he didn't. Surprise Lake?—it was Surprise Cabin to me. I had never heard of it before. I confess I was a bit tired. I had been looking for Lon to stop and make camp any time for an hour; but I had too much pride to suggest making camp or to ask him his intentions; and yet he was my man, hired at a handsome wage to mush my dogs for me and to obey my commands. I guess I was a bit grumpy myself. He said nothing, and I was resolved to ask nothing, even if we tramped on all night.

We came upon the cabin abruptly. For a week of trail we had met no one, and, in my mind, there had been little likelihood of meeting anyone for a week to come. And yet there it was, right before my eyes, a cabin, with a dim light in the window and smoke curling up from the chimney.

'Why didn't you tell me—' I began, but was interrupted by Lon, who muttered—

'Surprise Lake—it lies up a small feeder half a mile on. It's only a pond.'

'Yes, but the cabin—who lives in it?'

'A woman,' was the answer, and the next moment Lon had rapped on the door, and a woman's voice bade him enter.

'Have you seen Dave recently?' she asked.

'Nope,' Lon answered carelessly. 'I've been in the other direction, down Circle City way. Dave's up Dawson way, ain't he?'

The woman nodded, and Lon fell to unharnessing the dogs, while I unlashed the sled and carried the camp outfit into the cabin. The cabin was a large, one-room affair, and the woman was evidently alone in it. She pointed to the stove, where water was already boiling, and Lon set about the preparation of supper, while I opened the fish-bag and fed the dogs. I looked for Lon to introduce us, and was vexed that he did not, for they were evidently old friends.

'You are Lon McFane, aren't you?' I heard her ask him. 'Why, I remember you now. The last time I saw you it was on a steamboat, wasn't it? I remember...'

Her speech seemed suddenly to be frozen by the spectacle of dread which, I knew, from the terror I saw mounting in her eyes, must be on her inner vision. To my astonishment, Lon was affected by her words and manner. His face showed desperate, for all his voice sounded hearty and genial, as he said—

'The last time we met was at Dawson, Queen's Jubilee, or Birthday, or something—don't you remember?—the canoe races in the river, and the obstacle races down the main street?'

The terror faded out of her eyes and her whole body relaxed. 'Oh, yes, I do remember,' she said. 'And you won one of the canoe races.'

'How's Dave been makin' it lately? Strikin' it as rich as ever, I suppose?' Lon asked, with apparent irrelevance.

She smiled and nodded, and then, noticing that I had unlashed the bedroll, she indicated the end of the cabin where I might spread it. Her own bunk, I noticed, was made up at the opposite end.

'I thought it was Dave coming when I heard your dogs,' she said.

After that she said nothing, contenting herself with watching Lon's cooking operations, and listening the while as for the sound of dogs along the trail. I lay back on the blankets and smoked and watched. Here was mystery; I could make that much out, but no more could I make out. Why in the deuce hadn't Lon given me the tip before we arrived? I looked at her face, unnoticed by her, and the longer I looked the harder it was to take my eyes away. It was a wonderfully beautiful face, unearthly, I may say, with a light in it or an expression or something 'that was never on land or sea'. Fear and terror had completely vanished, and it was a placidly beautiful face—if by 'placid' one can characterize that intangible and occult something that I cannot say was a radiance or a light any more than I can say it was an expression.

Abruptly, as if for the first time, she became aware of my presence.

'Have you seen Dave recently?' she asked me. It was on the tip of my tongue to say 'Dave who?' when Lon coughed in the smoke that arose from the sizzling bacon. The bacon might have caused that cough, but I took it as a hint and left my question unasked. 'No, I haven't,' I answered. 'I'm new in this part of the country—'

'But you don't mean to say,' she interrupted, 'that you've never heard of Dave—of Big Dave Walsh?'

'You see,' I apologized, 'I'm new in the country. I've put in most of my time in the Lower Country, down Nome way.'

'Tell him about Dave,' she said to Lon.

Lon seemed put out, but he began in that hearty, genial manner that I had noticed before. It seemed a shade too hearty and genial, and it irritated me.

'Oh, Dave is a fine man,' he said. 'He's a man, every inch of him, and he stands six feet four in his socks. His word is as good as his bond. The man lies who ever says Dave told a lie, and that man will have to fight with me, too, as well—if there's anything left of him when Dave gets done with him. For Dave is a fighter. Oh, yes, he's a scrapper from way back. He got a grizzly with a '38 popgun. He got clawed some, but he knew what he was doin'. He went into the cave on purpose to get that grizzly. 'Fraid of nothing. Free an' easy with his money, or his last shirt an' match when out of money. Why, he drained Surprise Lake here in three weeks an' took out ninety thousand, didn't he?' She flushed and nodded her head proudly. Through his recital she had followed every word with keenest interest. 'An' I must say,' Lon went on, 'that I was disappointed sore on not meeting Dave here tonight.'

Lon served supper at one end of the table of whip-sawed spruce, and we fell to eating. A howling of the dogs took the woman to the door. She opened it an inch and listened.

'Where is Dave Walsh?' I asked, in an undertone.

'Dead,' Lon answered. 'In hell, maybe. I don't know. Shut up.'

'But you just said that you expected to meet him here tonight,' I challenged.

'Oh, shut up, can't you,' was Lon's reply, in the same cautious undertone.

The woman had closed the door and was returning, and I sat and meditated upon the fact that this man who told me to shut up received from me a salary of two hundred and fifty dollars a month and his board.

Lon washed the dishes, while I smoked and watched the woman. She seemed more beautiful than ever—strangely and weirdly beautiful, it is true. After looking at her steadfastly for five minutes, I was compelled to come back to the real world and to glance at Lon McFane. This enabled me to know, without discussion, that the woman, too, was real. At first I had taken her for the wife of Dave Walsh; but if Dave Walsh were dead, as Lon had said, then she could be only his widow.

It was early to bed, for we faced a long day on the morrow; and as Lon crawled in beside me under the blankets, I ventured a question.

'That woman's crazy, isn't she?'

'Crazy as a loon,' he answered.

And before I could formulate my next question, Lon McFane, I swear, was off to sleep. He always went to sleep that way—just crawled into the blankets, closed his eyes, and was off, a demure little heavy breathing rising on the air. Lon never snored.

And in the morning it was quick breakfast, feed the dogs, load the sled, and hit the trail. We said goodbye as we pulled out, and the woman stood in the doorway and watched us off. I carried the vision of her unearthly beauty away with me, just under my eyelids, and all I had to do, any time, was to close them and see her again. The way was unbroken, Surprise Lake being far off the travelled trails, and Lon and I took turn about at beating down the feathery snow with our big, webbed shoes so that the dogs could travel. 'But you said you expected to meet Dave Walsh at the cabin,' trembled on the tip of my tongue a score of times. I did not utter it. I could wait until we knocked off in the middle of the day. And when the middle of the day came, we went right on, for, as Lon explained, there was a camp of moose hunters at the forks of the Teelee, and we could make there by dark. But we didn't make there by dark, for Bright, the lead dog, broke his shoulder-blade, and we lost an hour over him before we shot him. Then, crossing a timber jam on the frozen bed of the Teelee, the sled suffered a wrenching capsize, and it was a case of make camp and repair the runner. I cooked supper and fed the dogs while Lon made the repairs, and together we got in the night's supply of ice and firewood. Then we sat on our blankets, our moccasins steaming on upended sticks before the fire, and had our evening smoke.

'You didn't know her?' Lon queried suddenly. I shook my head.

'You noticed the colour of her hair and eyes and her complexion, well, that's where she got her name—she was like the first warm glow of a golden sunrise. She was called Flush of Gold. Ever heard of her?'

Somewhere I had a confused and misty remembrance of having heard the name, yet it meant nothing to me. 'Flush of Gold,' I repeated, 'sounds like the name of a dance-house girl.'

Lon shook his head. 'No, she was a good woman, at least in that sense, though she sinned greatly just the same.'

'But why do you speak always of her in the past tense, as though she were dead?'

'Because of the darkness on her soul that is the same as the darkness of death. The Flush of Gold that I knew, that Dawson knew, and that Forty Mile knew before that, is dead. That dumb, lunatic creature we saw last night was not Flush of Gold.'

'And Dave?' I queried.

'He built that cabin,' Lon answered, 'He built it for her…and for himself. He is dead. She is waiting for him there. She half believes he is not dead. But who can know the whim of a crazed mind? Maybe she wholly believes he is not dead. At any rate, she waits for him there in the cabin he built. Who would rouse the dead? Then who would rouse the living that are dead? Not I, and that is why I let on to expect to meet Dave Walsh there last night. I'll bet a stack that I'd a been more surprised than she if I had met him there last night.'

'I do not understand,' I said. 'Begin at the beginning, as a white man should, and tell me the whole tale.'

And Lon began. 'Victor Chauvet was an old Frenchman—born in the south of France. He came to California in the days of gold. He was a pioneer. He found no gold, but, instead, became a maker of bottled sunshine—in short, a grape-grower and wine-maker. Also, he followed gold excitements. That is what brought him to Alaska in the early days, and over the Chilcoot and down the

Yukon long before the Carmack strike. The old town site of Ten Mile was Chauvet's. He carried the first mail into Arctic City. He staked those coal-mines on the Porcupine a dozen years ago. He grubstaked Loftus into the Nippennuck Country. Now it happened that Victor Chauvet was a good Catholic, loving two things in this world, wine and woman. Wine of all kinds he loved, but of woman, only one, and she was the mother of Marie Chauvet.'

Here I groaned aloud, having meditated beyond self-control over the fact that I paid this man two hundred and fifty dollars a month.

'What's the matter now?' he demanded.

'Matter?' I complained. 'I thought you were telling the story of Flush of Gold. I don't want a biography of your old French wine-bibber.'

Lon calmly lighted his pipe, took one good puff, then put the pipe aside. 'And you asked me to begin at the beginning,' he said.

'Yes,' said I, 'the beginning.'

'And the beginning of Flush of Gold is the old French wine-bibber, for he was the father of Marie Chauvet, and Marie Chauvet was the Flush of Gold. What more do you want? Victor Chauvet never had much luck to speak of. He managed to live, and to get along, and to take good care of Marie, who resembled the one woman he had loved. He took very good care of her. Flush of Gold was the pet name he gave her. Flush of Gold Creek was named after her—Flush of Gold town site, too. The old man was great on town sites, only he never landed them.

'Now, honestly,' Lon said, with one of his lightning changes, 'you've seen her, what do you think of her—of her looks, I mean? How does she strike your beauty sense?'

'She is remarkably beautiful,' I said. 'I never saw anything like her in my life. In spite of the fact, last night, that I guessed she was mad, I could not keep my eyes off of her. It wasn't curiosity. It was wonder, sheer wonder, she was so strangely beautiful.'

'She was more strangely beautiful before the darkness fell upon her,' Lon said softly. 'She was truly the Flush of Cold. She turned all men's hearts...and heads. She recalls, with an effort, that I once won a canoe race at Dawson—I, who once loved her, and was told by her of her love for me. It was her beauty that made all men love her. She'd got the apple from Paris, on application, and there wouldn't have been any Trojan War, and to top it off she'd have thrown Paris down. And now she lives in darkness, and she who was always fickle, for the first time is constant—and constant to a shade, to a dead man she does not realize is dead.

'And this is the way it was. You remember what I said last night of Dave Walsh—Big Dave Walsh? He was all that I said, and more, many times more. He came into this country in the late eighties—that's a pioneer for you. He was twenty years old then. He was a young bull. When he was twenty-five he could lift clear of the ground thirteen fifty-pound sacks of flour. At first, each fall of the year, famine drove him out. It was a lone land in those days. No river steamboats, no grub, nothing but salmon bellies and rabbit tracks. But after famine chased him out three years, he said he'd had enough of being chased; and the next year he stayed. He lived on straight meat when he was lucky enough to get it; he ate eleven dogs that winter; but he stayed. And the next winter he stayed, and the next. He never did leave the country again. He was a bull, a great bull. He could kill the strongest man in the country with hard work. He could outpack a Chilcat Indian, he could outpaddle a Stick, and he could travel all day with wet feet when the thermometer registered fifty below zero, and that's going some, I tell you, for vitality. You'd freeze your feet at twenty-five below if you wet them and tried to keep on.

'Dave Walsh was a bull for strength. And yet he was soft and easy-natured. Anybody could do him, the latest short-horn in camp could lie his last dollar out of him. "But it doesn't worry me," he had a way of laughing off his softness; "it doesn't keep me awake nights." Now don't get the idea that he had no backbone. You remember about the bear he went after with the popgun. When it came to fighting Dave was the blamedest ever. He was the limit, if by that I may describe his unlimitedness when he got into action. He was easy and kind with the weak, but the strong had to give trail when he went by. And he was a man that men liked, which is the finest word of all, a man's man.

'Dave never took part in the big stampede to Dawson when Carmack made the Bonanza strike. You see, Dave was just then over on Mammon Creek strikin' it himself. He discovered Mammon Creek. Cleaned eighty-four thousand up that winter, and opened up the claim so that it promised a couple of hundred thousand for the next winter. Then, summer bein' on and the ground sloshy, he took a trip up the Yukon to Dawson to see what Carmack's strike looked like. And there he saw Flush of Gold. I remember the night. I shall always remember. It was something sudden, and it makes one shiver to think of a strong man with all the strength withered out of him by one glance from the soft eyes of a weak, blond, female creature like Flush of Gold. It was at her dad's cabin, old Victor Chauvet's. Some friend had brought Dave along to talk over town sites on Mammon Creek. But little talking did he do, and what he did was mostly gibberish. I tell you the sight of Flush of Gold had sent Dave clean daffy. Old Victor Chauvet insisted after Dave left that he had been drunk. And so he had. He was drunk, but Flush of Gold was the strong drink that made him so.

'That settled it, that first glimpse he caught of her. He did not start back down the Yukon in a week, as he had intended. He lingered on a month, two months, all summer. And we who had suffered understood, and wondered what the outcome would be. Undoubtedly, in our minds, it seemed that Flush of Gold had met her master. And why not? There was romance sprinkled all over Dave Walsh. He was a Mammon King, he had made the Mammon Creek strike; he was an old sourdough, one of the oldest pioneers in the land—men turned to look at him when he went by, and said to one another in awed undertones, "There goes Dave Walsh." And why not? He stood six feet four; he had yellow hair himself that curled on his neck; and he was a bull—a yellow-maned bull just turned thirty-one.

'And Flush of Gold loved him, and, having danced him through a whole summer's courtship, at the end their engagement was made known. The fall of the year was at hand, Dave had to be back for the winter's work on Mammon Creek, and Flush of Gold refused to be married right away. Dave put Dusky Burns in charge of the Mammon Creek claim, and himself lingered on in Dawson. Little use. She wanted her freedom a while longer; she must have it, and she would not marry until next year. And so, on the first ice, Dave Walsh went alone down the Yukon behind his dogs, with the understanding that the marriage would take place when he arrived on the first steamboat of the next year.

'Now Dave was as true as the Pole Star, and she was as false as a magnetic needle in a cargo of loadstone. Dave was as steady and solid as she was fickle and flyaway, and in some way Dave, who never doubted anybody, doubted her. It was the jealousy of his love, perhaps, and maybe it was the message ticked off from her soul to his; but at any rate Dave was worried by fear of her inconstancy. He was afraid to trust her till the next year, he had so to trust her, and he was pretty well beside himself. Some of it I got from old Victor Chauvet afterwards, and from all that I have pieced together I conclude that there was something of a scene before Dave pulled north with his dogs. He stood up before the old Frenchman, with Flush of Gold beside him, and announced that they were plighted to each other. He was very dramatic, with fire in his eyes, old Victor said. He talked something about "until death do us part"; and old Victor especially remembered that at one place Dave took her by the shoulder with his great paw and almost shook her as he said: "Even unto death are you mine, and I would rise from the grave to claim you." Old Victor distinctly remembered those words "Even unto death are you mine, and I would rise from the grave to claim you." And he told me afterwards that Flush of Gold was pretty badly frightened, and that he afterwards took Dave to one side privately and told him that that wasn't the way to hold Flush of Gold—that he must humour her and gentle her if he wanted to keep her.

'There is no discussion in my mind but that Flush of Gold was frightened. She was a savage herself in her treatment of men, while men had always treated her as a soft and tender and too utterly-utter something that must not be hurt. She didn't know what harshness was...until Dave Walsh, standing his six feet four, a big bull, gripped her and pawed her and assured her that she was his until death, and then some. And besides, in Dawson, that winter, was a music-player—one of those macaroni-eating, greasy-tenor-Eyetalian-dago propositions—and Flush of Gold lost her heart to him. Maybe it was only fascination—I don't know. Sometimes it seems to me that she really did love Dave Walsh. Perhaps it was because he had frightened her with that even-unto-death, rise-from-the-grave stunt of his that she in the end inclined to the dago music-player. But it is all guesswork, and the facts are, sufficient. He wasn't a dago; he was a Russian count—this was straight; and he wasn't a professional piano-player or anything of the sort. He played the violin and the piano, and he sang—sang well—but it was for his own pleasure and for the pleasure of those he sang for. He had money, too—and right here let me say that Flush of Gold never cared a rap for money. She was fickle, but she was never sordid.

'But to be getting along. She was plighted to Dave, and Dave was coming up on the first steamboat to get her—that was the summer of '98, and the first steamboat was to be expected the middle of June. And Flush of Gold was afraid to throw Dave down and face him afterwards. It was all planned suddenly. The Russian music-player, the Count, was her obedient slave. She planned it, I know. I learned as much from old Victor afterwards. The Count took his orders from her, and caught that first steamboat down. It was the *Golden Rocket*. And so did Flush of Gold catch it. And so did I. I was going to Circle City, and I was flabbergasted when I found Flush of Gold on board. I didn't see her name down on the passenger list. She was with the Count fellow all the time, happy and smiling, and I noticed that the Count fellow was down on the list as having his wife along. There it was, stateroom, number, and all. The first I knew that he was married, only I didn't see anything of the wife…unless Flush of Gold was so counted. I wondered if they'd got married ashore before starting. There'd been talk about them in Dawson, you see, and bets had been laid that the Count fellow had cut Dave out.

'I talked with the purser. He didn't know anything more about it than I did; he didn't know Flush of Gold, anyway, and besides, he was almost rushed to death. You know what a Yukon steamboat is, but you can't guess what the *Golden Rocket* was when it left Dawson that June of 1898. She was a hummer. Being the first steamer out, she carried all the scurvy patients and hospital wrecks. Then she must have carried a couple of millions of Klondike dust and nuggets, to say nothing of a packed and jammed passenger list, deck passengers galore, and bucks and squaws and dogs without end. And she was loaded down to the guards with freight and baggage. There was a mountain of the same on the fore-lower deck, and each little stop along the way added to it. I saw the box come aboard at Teelee Portage, and I knew it for what it was, though I little guessed the joker that was in it. And they piled it on top of everything else on the fore-lower deck, and they didn't pile it any too securely either. The mate expected to come back to it again, and then forgot about it. I thought at the time that there was something familiar about the big husky dog that climbed over the baggage and freight and lay down next to the box. And then we passed the *Glendale*, bound up for Dawson. As she saluted us, I thought of Dave on board of her and hurrying to Dawson to Flush of Gold. I turned and looked at her where she stood by the rail. Her eyes were bright, but she looked a bit frightened by the sight of the other steamer, and she was leaning closely to the Count fellow as for protection. She needn't have leaned so safely against him, and I needn't have been so sure of a disappointed Dave Walsh arriving at Dawson. For Dave Walsh wasn't on the *Glendale*. There were a lot of things I didn't know, but was soon to know—for instance, that the pair were not yet married. Inside half an hour preparations for the marriage took place. What of the sick men in the main cabin, and of the crowded condition of the *Golden Rocket*, the likeliest place for the ceremony was found forward, on the lower deck, in an open space next to the rail and gangplank and shaded by the mountain of freight with the big box on top and the sleeping dog beside it. There was a missionary on board, getting off at Eagle City, which was the next step, so they had to use him quick. That's what they'd planned to do, get married on the boat.

'But I've run ahead of the facts. The reason Dave Walsh wasn't on the *Glendale* was because he was on the *Golden Rocket*. It was this way. After loiterin' in Dawson on account of Flush of Gold, he went down to Mammon Creek on the ice. And there he found Dusky Burns doing so well with the claim, there was no need for him to be around. So he put some grub on the sled, harnessed the dogs, took an Indian along, and pulled out for Surprise Lake. He always had a liking for that section. Maybe you don't know how the creek turned out to be a four-flusher; but the prospects were good at the time, and Dave proceeded to build his cabin and hers. That's the cabin we slept in. After he finished it, he went off on a moose hunt to the forks of the Teelee, takin' the Indian along.

'And this is what happened. Came on a cold snap. The juice went down forty, fifty, sixty below zero. I remember that snap—I was at Forty Mile; and I remember the very day. At eleven o'clock in the morning the spirit thermometer at the N.A.T.&T. Company's store went down to seventy-five below zero. And that morning, near the forks of the Teelee, Dave Walsh was out after moose with that blessed Indian of his. I got it all from the Indian afterwards—we made a trip over the ice together to Dyea. That morning Mr Indian broke through the ice and wet himself to the waist. Of course he began to freeze right away. The proper thing was to build a fire. But Dave Walsh was a bull. It was only half a mile to camp, where a fire was already burning. What was the good of building another? He threw Mr Indian over his shoulder—and ran with him—half a mile—with the thermometer at seventy-five below. You know what that means. Suicide. There's no other name for it. Why, that buck Indian weighed over two hundred himself, and Dave ran half a mile with him. Of course he froze his lungs. Must have frozen them near solid. It was a tomfool trick for any man to do. And anyway, after lingering horribly for several weeks, Dave Walsh died.

'The Indian didn't know what to do with the corpse. Ordinarily he'd have buried him and let it go at that. But he knew that Dave Walsh was a big man, worth lots of money, a hi-yu skookum chief. Likewise he'd seen the bodies of other hi-yu skookums carted around the country like they were worth something. So he decided to take Dave's body to Forty Mile, which was Dave's headquarters. You know how the ice is on the grass roots in this country—well, the Indian planted Dave under a foot of soil—in short, he put Dave on ice. Dave could have stayed there a thousand years and still been the same old Dave. You understand—just the same as a refrigerator. Then the Indian brings over a whipsaw from the cabin at Surprise Lake and makes lumber enough for the box. Also, waiting for the thaw, he goes out and shoots about ten thousand pounds of moose. This he keeps on ice, too. Came the thaw. The Teelee broke. He built a raft and loaded it with the meat, the big box with Dave inside, and Dave's team of dogs, and away they went down the Teelee.

'The raft got caught on a timber jam and hung up two days. It was scorching hot weather, and Mr Indian nearly lost his moose meat. So when he got to Teelee Portage he figured a steamboat would get to Forty Mile quicker than his raft. He transferred his cargo, and there you are, fore-lower deck of the *Golden Rocket*, Flush of Gold being married, and Dave Walsh in his big box casting the shade for her. And there's one thing I clean forgot. No wonder I thought the husky dog that came aboard at Teelee Portage was familiar. It was Pee-lat, Dave Walsh's lead dog and favourite—a terrible fighter, too. He was lying down beside the box.

'Flush of Gold caught sight of me, called me over, shook hands with me, and introduced me to the Count. She was beautiful. I was as mad for her then as ever. She smiled into my eyes and said I must sign as one of the witnesses. And there was no refusing her. She was ever a child, cruel as children are cruel. Also, she told me she was in possession of the only two bottles of champagne in Dawson—or that had been in Dawson the night before; and before I knew it I was scheduled to drink to her and the Count's health. Everybody crowded round, the captain of the steamboat, very prominent, trying to ring in on the wine, I guess. It was a funny wedding. On the upper deck the hospital wrecks, with various feet in the grave, gathered and looked down to see. There were Indians all jammed in the circle, too, big bucks, and their squaws and kids, to say nothing of about twenty-five snarling wolf-dogs. The missionary lined the two of them up and started in with the service. And just then a dog-fight started, high up on the pile of freight—Pee-lat lying beside the big box, and a white-haired brute belonging to one of the Indians. The fight wasn't explosive at all. The brutes just snarled at each other from a distance—tapping at each other long-distance, you know, saying dast and dassent, dast and dassent. The noise was rather disturbing, but you could hear the missionary's voice above it.

'There was no particularly easy way of getting at the two dogs, except from the other side of the pile. But nobody was on that side—everybody watching the ceremony, you see. Even then everything might have been all right if the captain hadn't thrown a club at the dogs. That was what precipitated everything. As I say, if the captain hadn't thrown that club, nothing might have happened.

'The missionary had just reached the point where he was saying "In sickness and in health," and "Till death us do part." And just then the captain threw the club. I saw the whole thing. It landed on Pee-lat, and at that instant the white brute jumped him. The club caused it. Their two bodies struck the box, and it began to slide, its lower end tilting down. It was a long oblong box, and it slid down slowly until it reached the perpendicular, when it came down on the run. The onlookers on that side of the circle had time to get out from under. Flush of Gold and the Count, on the opposite side of the circle, were facing the box; the missionary had his back to it. The box must have fallen ten feet straight up and down, and it hit end on.

'Now mind you, not one of us knew that Dave Walsh was dead. We thought he was on the *Glendale*, bound for Dawson. The missionary had edged off to one side, and so Flush of Gold faced the box when it struck. It was like in a play. It couldn't have been better planned. It struck on end, and on the right end; the whole front of the box came off; and out swept Dave Walsh on his feet, partly wrapped in a blanket, his yellow hair flying and showing bright in the sun. Right out of the box, on his feet, he swept upon Flush of Gold. She didn't know he was dead, but it was unmistakable, after hanging up two days on a timber jam, that he was rising all right from the dead to claim her. Possibly that is what she thought. At any rate, the sight froze her. She couldn't move. She just sort of wilted and watched Dave Walsh coming for her! And he got her. It looked almost as though he threw his arms around her, but whether or not this happened, down to the deck they went together. We had to drag Dave Walsh's body clear before we could get hold of her. She was in a faint, but it would have been just as well if she had never come out of that faint; for when she did, she fell to screaming the way insane people do. She kept it up for hours, till she was exhausted. Oh, yes, she recovered. You saw her last night, and know how much recovered she is. She is not violent, it is true, but she lives in darkness. She believes that she is waiting for Dave Walsh, and so she waits in the cabin he built for her. She is no longer fickle. It is nine years now that she has been faithful to Dave Walsh, and the outlook is that she'll be faithful to him to the end.'

Lon McFane pulled down the top of the blankets and prepared to crawl in.

'We have her grub hauled to her each year,' he added, 'and in general keep an eye on her. Last night was the first time she ever recognized me, though.'

'Who are the *we*?' I asked.

'Oh,' was the answer, 'the Count and old Victor Chauvet and me. Do you know, I think the Count is the one to be really sorry for. Dave Walsh never did know that she was false to him. And she does not suffer. Her darkness is merciful to her.'

I lay silently under the blankets for the space of a minute.

'Is the Count still in the country?' I asked.

But there was a gentle sound of heavy breathing, and I knew Lon McFane was asleep.

4

FOUR HORSES AND A SAILOR

'Huh! Drive four horses! I wouldn't sit behind you—not for a thousand dollars—over them mountain roads.'

So said Henry, and he ought to have known, for he drives four horses himself.

Said another Glen Ellen friend: 'What? London? He drive four horses? Can't drive one!'

And the best of it is that he was right. Even after managing to get a few hundred miles with my four horses, I don't know how to drive one. Just the other day, swinging down a steep mountain road and rounding an abrupt turn, I came full tilt on a horse and buggy being driven by a woman up the hill. We could not pass on the narrow road, where was only a foot to spare, and my horses did not know how to back, especially uphill. About two hundred yards down the hill was a spot where we could pass. The driver of the buggy said she didn't dare back down because she was not sure of the brake. And as I didn't know how to tackle one horse, I didn't try it. So we unhitched her horse and backed down by hand. Which was very well, till it came to hitching the horse to the buggy again. She didn't know how. I didn't either, and I had depended on her knowledge. It took us about half an hour, with frequent debates and consultations, though it is an absolute certainty that never in its life was that horse hitched in that particular way.

No; I can't harness up one horse. But I can four, which compels me to back up again to get to my beginning. Having selected Sonoma Valley for our abiding place, Charmian and I decided it was about time we knew what we had in our own county and the neighbouring ones. How to do it, was the first question. Among our many weaknesses is the one of being old-fashioned. We don't mix with gasolene very well. And, as true sailors should, we naturally gravitate toward horses. Being one of those lucky individuals who carries his office under his hat, I should have to take a typewriter and a load of books along. This put saddle-horses out of the running. Charmian suggested driving a span. She had faith in me; besides, she could drive a span herself. But when I thought of the many mountains to cross, and of crossing them for three months with a poor tired span, I vetoed the proposition and said we'd have to come back to gasolene after all. This she vetoed just as emphatically, and a deadlock obtained until I received inspiration.

'Why not drive four horses?' I said.

'But you don't know how to drive four horses,' was her objection.

I threw my chest out and my shoulders back. 'What man has done, I can do,' I proclaimed grandly. 'And please don't forget that when we sailed on the *Snark* I knew nothing of navigation, and that I taught myself as I sailed.'

'Very well,' she said. (And there's faith for you!) 'They shall be four saddle horses, and we'll strap our saddles on behind the rig.'

It was my turn to object. 'Our saddle-horses are not broken to harness.'

'Then break them.'

And what I knew about horses, much less about breaking them, was just about as much as any sailor knows. Having been kicked, bucked off, fallen over backward upon, and thrown out and run over, on very numerous occasions, I had a mighty vigorous respect for horses; but a wife's faith must be lived up to, and I went at it.

King was a polo pony from St. Louis, and Prince a many-gaited love-horse from Pasadena. The hardest thing was to get them to dig in and pull. They rollicked along on the levels and galloped down the hills, but when they struck an upgrade and felt the weight of the breaking-cart, they stopped and turned around and looked at me. But I passed them, and my troubles began. Milda was fourteen years old, an unadulterated broncho, and in temperament was a combination of mule and jack-rabbit blended equally. If you pressed your hand on her flank and told her to get over, she lay down on you. If you got her by the head and told her to back, she walked forward over you. And if you got behind her and shoved and told her to 'Giddap!' she sat down on you. Also, she wouldn't walk. For endless weary miles I strove with her, but never could I get her to walk a step. Finally, she was a manger-glutton. No matter how near or far from the stable, when six o'clock came around she bolted for home and never missed the directest crossroad. Many times I rejected her.

The fourth and most rejected horse of all was the Outlaw. From the age of three to seven she had defied all horse-breakers and broken a number of them. Then a long, lanky cowboy, with a fifty-pound saddle and a Mexican bit had got her proud goat. I was the next owner. She was my favourite riding horse. Charmian said I'd have to put her in as a wheeler where I would have more control over her. Now Charmian had a favourite riding mare called Maid. I suggested Maid as a substitute. Charmian pointed out that my mare was a branded range horse, while hers was a near-thoroughbred, and that the legs of her mare would be ruined forever if she were driven for three months. I acknowledged her mare's thoroughbredness, and at the same time defied her to find any thoroughbred with as small and delicately-viciously pointed ears as my Outlaw. She indicated Maid's exquisitely thin shinbone.

I measured the Outlaw's. It was equally thin, although, I insinuated, possibly more durable. This stabbed Charmian's pride. Of course her near-thoroughbred Maid, carrying the blood of 'old' Lexington, Morella, and a streak of the super-enduring Morgan, could run, walk, and work my unregistered Outlaw into the ground; and that was the very precise reason why such a paragon of a saddle animal should not be degraded by harness.

So it was that Charmian remained obdurate, until, one day, I got her behind the Outlaw for a forty-mile drive. For every inch of those forty miles the Outlaw kicked and jumped, in between the kicks and jumps finding time and space in which to seize its team-mate by the back of the neck and attempt to drag it to the ground. Another trick the Outlaw developed during that drive was suddenly to turn at right angles in the traces and endeavour to butt its team-mate over the grade. Reluctantly and nobly did Charmian give in and consent to the use of Maid. The Outlaw's shoes were pulled off, and she was turned out on range.

Finally, the four horses were hooked to the rig—a light Studebaker trap. With two hours and a half of practice, in which the excitement was not abated by several jack-poles and numerous kicking matches, I announced myself as ready for the start. Came the morning, and Prince, who was to have been a wheeler with Maid, showed up with a badly kicked shoulder. He did not exactly show up; we had to find him, for he was unable to walk. His leg swelled and continually swelled during the several days we waited for him. Remained only the Outlaw. In from pasture she came, shoes were nailed on, and she was harnessed into the wheel. Friends and relatives strove to press accident policies on me, but Charmian climbed up alongside, and Nakata got into the rear seat with the typewriter—Nakata, who sailed cabin-boy on the *Snark* for two years and who had shown himself afraid of nothing, not even of me and my amateur jamborees in experimenting with new modes of locomotion. And we did very nicely, thank you, especially after the first hour or so, during which time the Outlaw had kicked about fifty various times, chiefly to the damage of her own legs and the paintwork, and after she had bitten a couple of hundred times, to the damage of Maid's neck and Charmian's temper. It was hard enough to have her favourite mare in the harness without also enduring the spectacle of its being eaten alive.

Our leaders were joys. King being a polo pony and Milda a rabbit, they rounded curves beautifully and darted ahead like coyotes out of the way of the wheelers. Milda's besetting weakness was a frantic desire not to have the lead-bar strike her hocks. When this happened, one of three things occurred: either she sat down on the lead-bar, kicked it up in the air until she got her back under it, or exploded in a straight-ahead, harness-disrupting jump. Not until she carried the lead-bar clean away and danced a breakdown on it and the traces, did she behave decently. Nakata and I made the repairs with good old-fashioned bale-rope, which is stronger than wrought iron any time, and we went on our way.

In the meantime I was learning—I shall not say to tool a four-in-hand—but just simply to drive four horses. Now it is all right enough to begin with four work-horses pulling a load of several tons. But to begin with four light horses, all running, and a light rig that seems to outrun them—well, when things happen they happen quickly. My weakness was total ignorance. In particular, my fingers lacked training, and I made the mistake of depending on my eyes to handle the reins. This brought me up against a disastrous optical illusion. The bight of the off head-line, being longer and heavier than that of the off wheel-line, hung lower. In a moment requiring quick action, I invariably mistook the two lines. Pulling on what I thought was the wheel-line, in order to straighten the team, I would see the leaders swing abruptly around into a jack-pole. Now for sensations of sheer impotence, nothing can compare with a jack-pole, when the horrified driver beholds his leaders prancing gaily up the road and his wheelers jogging steadily down the road, all at the same time and all harnessed together and to the same rig.

I no longer jack-pole, and I don't mind admitting how I got out of the habit. It was my eyes that enslaved my fingers into ill practices. So I shut my eyes and let the fingers go it alone. Today my fingers are independent of my eyes and work automatically. I do not see what my fingers do. They just do it. All I see is the satisfactory result.

Still we managed to get over the ground that first day—down sunny Sonoma Valley to the old town of Sonoma, founded by General Vallejo as the remotest outpost on the northern frontier for the purpose of holding back the Gentiles, as the wild Indians of those days were called. Here history was made. Here the last Spanish mission was reared; here the Bear flag was raised; and here Kit Carson, and Fremont, and all our early adventurers came and rested in the days before the days of gold.

We swung on over the low, rolling hills, through miles of dairy farms and chicken ranches where every blessed hen is white, and down the slopes to Petaluma Valley. Here, in 1776, Captain Quiros came up Petaluma Creek from San Pablo Bay in quest of an outlet to Bodega Bay on the coast. And here, later, the Russians, with Alaskan hunters, carried skin boats across from Fort Ross to poach for sea-otters on the Spanish preserve of San Francisco Bay. Here, too, still later, General Vallejo built a fort, which still stands—one of the finest examples of Spanish adobe that remain to us. And here, at the old fort, to bring the chronicle up to date, our horses proceeded to make peculiarly personal history with astonishing success and dispatch. King, our peerless, polo-pony leader, went lame. So hopelessly lame did he go that no expert, then and afterward, could determine whether the lameness was in his frogs, hoofs, legs, shoulders, or head. Maid picked up a nail and began to limp. Milda, figuring the day already sufficiently spent and maniacal with manger-gluttony, began to rabbit-jump. All that held her was the bale-rope. And the Outlaw, game to the last, exceeded all previous exhibitions of skin-removing, paint-marring, and horse-eating.

At Petaluma we rested over while King was returned to the ranch and Prince sent to us. Now Prince had proved himself an excellent wheeler, yet he had to go into the lead and let the Outlaw retain his old place. There is an axiom that a good wheeler is a poor leader. I object to the last adjective. A good wheeler makes an infinitely worse kind of a leader than that. I know…now. I ought to know. Since that day I have driven Prince a few hundred miles in the lead. He is neither any better nor any worse than the first mile he ran in the lead; and his worst is even extremely worse than what you are thinking. Not that he is vicious. He is merely a good-natured rogue who shakes hands for sugar, steps on your toes out of sheer excessive friendliness, and just goes on loving you in your harshest moments.

But he won't get out of the way. Also, whenever he is reproved for being in the wrong, he accuses Milda of it and bites the back of her neck. So bad has this become that whenever I yell 'Prince!' in a loud voice, Milda immediately rabbit-jumps to the side, straight ahead, or sits down on the lead-bar. All of which is quite disconcerting. Picture it yourself. You are swinging round a sharp, downgrade, mountain curve, at a fast trot. The rock wall is the outside of the curve. The inside of the curve is a precipice. The continuance of the curve is a narrow, unrailed bridge. You hit the curve, throwing the leaders in against the wall and making the polo-horse do the work. All is lovely. The leaders are hugging the wall like nestling doves. But the moment comes in the evolution when the leaders must shoot out ahead. They really must shoot, or else they'll hit the wall and miss the bridge. Also, behind them are the wheelers, and the rig, and you have just eased the brake in order to put sufficient snap into the manoeuvre. If ever team-work is required, now is the time. Milda tries to shoot. She does her best, but Prince, bubbling over with roguishness, lags behind. He knows the trick. Milda is half a length ahead of him. He times it to the fraction of a second. Maid, in the wheel, over-running him, naturally bites him. This disturbs the Outlaw, who has been behaving beautifully, and she immediately reaches across for Maid. Simultaneously, with a fine display of firm conviction that it's all Milda's fault, Prince sinks his teeth into the back of Milda's defenceless neck. The whole thing has occurred in less than a second. Under the surprise and pain of the bite, Milda either jumps ahead to the imminent peril of harness and lead-bar, or smashes into the wall, stops short with the lead-bar over her back, and emits a couple of hysterical kicks. The Outlaw invariably selects this moment to remove paint. And after things are untangled and you have had time to appreciate the close shave, you go up to Prince and reprove him with your choicest vocabulary. And Prince, gazelle-eyed and tender, offers to shake hands with you for sugar. I leave it to any one: a boat would never act that way.

We have some history north of the Bay. Nearly three centuries and a half ago, that doughty pirate and explorer, Sir Francis Drake, combing the Pacific for Spanish galleons, anchored in the bight formed by Point Reyes, on which today is one of the richest dairy regions in the world. Here, less than two decades after Drake, Sebastien Carmenon piled up on the rocks with a silk-laden galleon from the Philippines. And in this same bay of Drake, long afterward, the Russian fur-poachers rendezvous'd their bidarkas and stole in through the Golden Gate to the forbidden waters of San Francisco Bay.

Farther up the coast, in Sonoma County, we pilgrimaged to the sites of the Russian settlements. At Bodega Bay, south of what today is called Russian River, was their anchorage, while north of the river they built their fort. And much of Fort Ross still stands. Log-bastions, church, and stables hold their own, and so well, with rusty hinges creaking, that we warmed ourselves at the hundred-years-old double fireplace and slept under the hand-hewn roof beams still held together by spikes of hand-wrought iron.

We went to see where history had been made, and we saw scenery as well. One of our stretches in a day's drive was from beautiful Inverness on Tomales Bay, down the Olema Valley to Bolinas Bay, along the eastern shore of that body of water to Willow Camp, and up over the sea-bluffs, around the bastions of Tamalpais, and down to Sausalito. From the head of Bolinas Bay to Willow Camp the drive on the edge of the beach, and actually, for half-mile stretches, in the waters of the bay itself, was a delightful experience. The wonderful part was to come. Very few San Franciscans, much less Californians, know of that drive from Willow Camp, to the south and east, along the poppy-blown cliffs, with the sea thundering in the sheer depths hundreds of feet below and the Golden Gate opening up ahead, disclosing smoky San Francisco on her many hills. Far off, blurred on the breast of the sea, can be seen the Farallones, which Sir Francis Drake passed on a S.W. course in the thick of what he describes as a 'stynking fog.' Well might he call it that, and a few other names, for it was the fog that robbed him of the glory of discovering San Francisco Bay.

It was on this part of the drive that I decided at last I was learning real mountain-driving. To confess the truth, for delicious titillation of one's nerve, I have since driven over no mountain road that was worse, or better, rather, than that piece.

And then the contrast! From Sausalito, over excellent, park-like boulevards, through the splendid redwoods and homes of Mill Valley, across the blossomed hills of Marin County, along the knoll-studded picturesque marshes, past San Rafael resting warmly among her hills, over the divide and up the Petaluma Valley, and on to the grassy feet of Sonoma Mountain and home. We covered fifty-five miles that day. Not so bad, eh, for Prince the Rogue, the paint-removing Outlaw, the thin-shanked thoroughbred, and the rabbit-jumper? And they came in cool and dry, ready for their mangers and the straw.

Oh, we didn't stop. We considered we were just starting, and that was many weeks ago. We have kept on going over six counties which are comfortably large, even for California, and we are still going. We have twisted and tabled, criss-crossed our tracks, made fascinating and lengthy dives into the interior valleys in the hearts of Napa and Lake Counties, travelled the coast for hundreds of miles on end, and are now in Eureka, on Humboldt Bay, which was discovered by accident by the gold-seekers, who were trying to find their way to and from the Trinity diggings. Even here, the white man's history preceded them, for dim tradition says that the Russians once anchored here and hunted sea-otter before the first Yankee trader rounded the Horn, or the first Rocky Mountain trapper thirsted across the 'Great American Desert' and trickled down the snowy Sierras to the sun-kissed land. No; we are not resting our horses here on Humboldt Bay. We are writing this article, gorging on abalones and mussels, digging clams, and catching record-breaking sea-trout and rock-cod in the intervals in which we are not sailing, motor-boating, and swimming in the most temperately equable climate we have ever experienced.

These comfortably large counties! They are veritable empires. Take Humboldt, for instance. It is three times as large as Rhode Island, one and a half times as large as Delaware, almost as large as Connecticut, and half as large as Massachusetts. The pioneer has done his work in this north of the bay region, the foundations are laid, and all is ready for the inevitable inrush of population and adequate development of resources which so far have been no more than skimmed, and casually and carelessly skimmed at that. This region of the six counties alone will some day support a population of millions. In the meanwhile, O you home-seekers, you wealth-seekers, and, above all, you climate-seekers, now is the time to get in on the ground floor.

Robert Ingersoll once said that the genial climate of California would in a fairly brief time evolve a race resembling the Mexicans, and that in two or three generations the Californians would be seen of a Sunday morning on their way to a cockfight with a rooster under each arm. Never was made a rasher generalization, based on so absolute an ignorance of facts. It is to laugh. Here is a climate that breeds vigour, with just sufficient geniality to prevent the expenditure of most of that vigour in fighting the elements. Here is a climate where a man can work three hundred and sixty-five days in the year without the slightest hint of enervation, and where for three hundred and sixty-five nights he must perforce sleep under blankets. What more can one say? I consider myself somewhat of a climate expert, having adventured among most of the climates of five out of the six zones. I have not yet been in the Antarctic, but whatever climate obtains there will not deter me from drawing the conclusion that nowhere is there a climate to compare with that of this region. Maybe I am as wrong as Ingersoll was. Nevertheless I take my medicine by continuing to live in this climate. Also, it is the only medicine I ever take.

But to return to the horses. There is some improvement. Milda has actually learned to walk. Maid has proved her thoroughbredness by never tiring on the longest days, and, while being the strongest and highest spirited of all, by never causing any trouble save for an occasional kick at the Outlaw. And the Outlaw rarely gallops, no longer butts, only periodically kicks, comes in to the pole and does her work without attempting to vivisect Maid's medulla oblongata, and—marvel of marvels—is really and truly getting lazy. But Prince remains the same incorrigible, loving and lovable rogue he has always been.

And the country we've been over! The drives through Napa and Lake Counties! One, from Sonoma Valley, via Santa Rosa, we could not refrain from taking several ways, and on all the ways we found the roads excellent for machines as well as horses. One route, and a more delightful one for an automobile cannot be found, is out from Santa Rosa, past old Altruria and Mark West Springs, then to the right and across to Calistoga in Napa Valley. By keeping to the left, the drive holds on up the Russian River Valley, through the miles of the noted Asti Vineyards to Cloverdale, and then by way of Pieta, Witter, and Highland Springs to Lakeport. Still another way we took, was down Sonoma Valley, skirting San Pablo Bay, and up the lovely Napa Valley. From Napa were side excursions through Pope and Berryessa Valleys, on to Aetna Springs, and still on, into Lake County, crossing the famous Langtry Ranch.

Continuing up the Napa Valley, walled on either hand by great rock palisades and redwood forests and carpeted with endless vineyards, and crossing the many stone bridges for which the County is noted and which are a joy to the beauty-loving eyes as well as to the four-horse tyro driver, past Calisttoga with its old mud-baths and chicken-soup springs, with St. Helena and its giant saddle ever towering before us, we climbed the mountains on a good grade and dropped down past the quicksilver mines to the canyon of the Geysers. After a stopover night and an exploration of the miniature-grand volcanic scene, we pulled on across the canyon and took the grade where the cicadas simmered audibly in the noon sunshine among the hillside manzanitas. Then, higher, came the big cattle-dotted upland pastures, and the rocky summit. And here on the summit, abruptly, we caught a vision, or what seemed a mirage. The ocean we had left long days before, yet far down and away shimmered a blue sea, framed on the farther shore by rugged mountains, on the near shore by fat and rolling farm lands. Clear Lake was before us, and like proper sailors we returned to our sea, going for a sail, a fish, and a swim ere the day was done and turning into tired Lakeport blankets in the early evening. Well has Lake County been called the Walled-in County.

But the railroad is coming. They say the approach we made to Clear Lake is similar to the approach to Lake Lucerne. Be that as it may, the scenery, with its distant snow-capped peaks, can well be called Alpine.

And what can be more exquisite than the drive out from Clear Lake to Ukiah by way of the Blue Lakes chain!—every turn bringing into view a picture of breathless beauty; every glance backward revealing some perfect composition in line and colour, the intense blue of the water margined with splendid oaks, green fields, and swaths of orange poppies. But those side glances and backward glances were provocative of trouble. Charmian and I disagreed as to which way the connecting stream of water ran. We still disagree, for at the hotel, where we submitted the affair to arbitration, the hotel manager and the clerk likewise disagreed. I assume, now, that we never will know which way that stream runs. Charmian suggests 'both ways'. I refuse such a compromise. No stream of water I ever saw could accomplish that feat at one and the same time. The greatest concession I can make is that sometimes it may run one way and sometimes the other, and that in the meantime we should both consult an oculist.

More valley from Ukiah to Willits, and then we turned westward through the virgin Sherwood Forest of magnificent redwood, stopping at Alpine for the night and continuing on through Mendocino County to Fort Bragg and 'salt water'. We also came to Fort Bragg up the coast from Fort Ross, keeping our coast journey intact from the Golden Gate. The coast weather was cool and delightful, the coast driving superb. Especially in the Fort Ross section did we find the roads thrilling, while all the way along we followed the sea. At every stream, the road skirted dizzy cliff-edges, dived down into lush growths of forest and ferns and climbed out along the cliff-edges again. The way was lined with flowers—wild lilac, wild roses, poppies, and lupins. Such lupins!—giant clumps of them, of every lupin-shade and colour. And it was along the Mendocino roads that Charmian caused many delays by insisting on getting out to pick the wild blackberries, strawberries, and thimble-berries which grew so profusely. And ever we caught peeps, far down, of steam schooners loading lumber in the rocky coves; ever we skirted the cliffs, day after day, crossing stretches of rolling farm lands and passing through thriving villages and saw-mill towns. Memorable was our launch-trip from Mendocino City up Big River, where the steering gears of the launches work the reverse of anywhere else in the world; where we saw a stream of logs, of six to twelve and fifteen feet in diameter, which filled the river bed for miles to the obliteration of any sign of water; and where we were told of a white or albino redwood tree. We did not see this last, so cannot vouch for it.

All the streams were filled with trout, and more than once we saw the side-hill salmon on the slopes. No, side-hill salmon is not a peripatetic fish; it is a deer out of season. But the trout! At Gualala Charmian caught her first one. Once before in my life I had caught two…on angleworms. On occasion I had tried fly and spinner and never got a strike, and I had come to believe that all this talk of fly-fishing was just so much nature-faking. But on the Gualala River I caught trout—a lot of them—on fly and spinners; and I was beginning to feel quite an expert, until Nakata, fishing on bottom with a pellet of bread for bait, caught the biggest trout of all. I now affirm there is nothing in science nor in art. Nevertheless, since that day poles and baskets have been added to our baggage, we tackle every stream we come to, and we no longer are able to remember the grand total of our catch.

At Usal, many hilly and picturesque miles north of Fort Bragg, we turned again into the interior of Mendocino, crossing the ranges and coming out in Humboldt County on the south fork of Eel River at Garberville. Throughout the trip, from Marin County north, we had been warned of 'bad roads ahead'. Yet we never found those bad roads. We seemed always to be just ahead of them or behind them. The farther we came the better the roads seemed, though this was probably due to the fact that we were learning more and more what four horses and a light rig could do on a road. And thus do I save my face with all the counties. I refuse to make invidious road comparisons. I can add that while, save in rare instances on steep pitches, I have trotted my horses down all the grades, I have never had one horse fall down nor have I had to send the rig to a blacksmith shop for repairs.

Also, I am learning to throw leather. If any tyro thinks it is easy to take a short-handled, long-lashed whip, and throw the end of that lash just where he wants it, let him put on automobile goggles and try it. On reconsideration, I would suggest the substitution of a wire fencing-mask for the goggles. For days I looked at that whip. It fascinated me, and the fascination was composed mostly of fear. At my first attempt, Charmian and Nakata became afflicted with the same sort of fascination, and for a long time afterward, whenever they saw me reach for the whip, they closed their eyes and shielded their heads with their arms.

Here's the problem. Instead of pulling honestly, Prince is lagging back and manoeuvring for a bite at Milda's neck. I have four reins in my hands. I must put these four reins into my left hand, properly gather the whip handle and the bight of the lash in my right hand, and throw that lash past Maid without striking her and into Prince. If the lash strikes Maid, her thoroughbredness will go up in the air, and I'll have a case of horse hysteria on my hands for the next half hour. But follow. The whole problem is not yet stated. Suppose that I miss Maid and reach the intended target. The instant the lash cracks, the four horses jump, Prince most of all, and his jump, with spread wicked teeth, is for the back of Milda's neck. She jumps to escape—which is her second jump, for the first one came when the lash exploded. The Outlaw reaches for Maid's neck, and Maid, who has already jumped and tried to bolt, tries to bolt harder. And all this infinitesimal fraction of time I am trying to hold the four animals with my left hand, while my whiplash, writhing through the air, is coming back to me. Three simultaneous things I must do: keep hold of the four reins with my left hand; slam on the brake with my foot; and on the rebound catch that flying lash in the hollow of my right arm and get the bight of it safely into my right hand. Then I must get two of the four lines back into my right hand and keep the horses from running away or going over the grade. Try it some time. You will find life anything but wearisome. Why, the first time I hit the mark and made the lash go off like a revolver shot, I was so astounded and delighted that I was paralyzed. I forgot to do any of the multitudinous other things, tangled the whiplash in Maid's harness, and was forced to call upon Charmian for assistance. And now, confession. I carry a few pebbles handy. They're great for reaching Prince in a tight place. But just the same I'm learning that whip every day, and before I get home I hope to discard the pebbles. And as long as I rely on pebbles, I cannot truthfully speak of myself as 'tooling a four-in-hand'.

From Garberville, where we ate eel to repletion and got acquainted with the aborigines, we drove down the Eel River Valley for two days through the most unthinkably glorious body of redwood timber to be seen anywhere in California. From Dyerville on to Eureka, we caught glimpses of railroad construction and of great concrete bridges in the course of building, which advertised that at least Humboldt County was going to be linked to the rest of the world.

We still consider our trip is just begun. As soon as this is mailed from Eureka, it's heigh ho! for the horses and pull on. We shall continue up the coast, turn in for Hoopa Reservation and the gold mines, and shoot down the Trinity and Klamath rivers in Indian canoes to Requa. After that, we shall go on through Del Norte County and into Oregon. The trip so far has justified us in taking the attitude that we won't go home until the winter rains drive us in. And, finally, I am going to try the experiment of putting Outlaw in the lead and relegating Prince to his old position in the near wheel. I won't need any pebbles then.

5

LOVE OF LIFE

'This out of all will remain—
They have lived and have tossed:
So much of the game will be gain,
Though the gold of the dice has been lost.'

They limped painfully down the bank, and once the foremost of the two men staggered among the rough-strewn rocks. They were tired and weak, and their faces had the drawn expression of patience which comes of hardship long endured. They were heavily burdened with blanket packs which were strapped to their shoulders. Head-straps, passing across the forehead, helped support these packs. Each man carried a rifle. They walked in a stooped posture, the shoulders well forward, the head still farther forward, the eyes bent upon the ground.

'I wish we had just about two of them cartridges that's layin' in that cache of ourn,' said the second man.

His voice was utterly and drearily expressionless. He spoke without enthusiasm; and the first man, limping into the milky stream that foamed over the rocks, vouchsafed no reply.

The other man followed at his heels. They did not remove their footgear, though the water was icy cold—so cold that their ankles ached and their feet went numb. In places the water dashed against their knees, and both men staggered for footing.

The man who followed slipped on a smooth boulder, nearly fell, but recovered himself with a violent effort, at the same time uttering a sharp exclamation of pain. He seemed faint and dizzy and put out his free hand while he reeled, as though seeking support against the air. When he had steadied himself he stepped forward, but reeled again and nearly fell. Then he stood still and looked at the other man, who had never turned his head.

The man stood still for fully a minute, as though debating with himself. Then he called out:

'I say, Bill, I've sprained my ankle.'

Bill staggered on through the milky water. He did not look around. The man watched him go, and though his face was expressionless as ever, his eyes were like the eyes of a wounded deer.

The other man limped up the farther bank and continued straight on without looking back. The man in the stream watched him. His lips trembled a little, so that the rough thatch of brown hair which covered them was visibly agitated. His tongue even strayed out to moisten them.

'Bill!' he cried out.

It was the pleading cry of a strong man in distress, but Bill's head did not turn. The man watched him go, limping grotesquely and lurching forward with stammering gait up the slow slope toward the soft skyline of the low-lying hill. He watched him go till he passed over the crest and disappeared. Then he turned his gaze and slowly took in the circle of the world that remained to him now that Bill was gone.

Near the horizon the sun was smouldering dimly, almost obscured by formless mists and vapours, which gave an impression of mass and density without outline or tangibility. The man pulled out his watch, the while resting his weight on one leg. It was four o'clock, and as the season was near the last of July or first of

August—he did not know the precise date within a week or two—he knew that the sun roughly marked the northwest. He looked to the south and knew that somewhere beyond those bleak hills lay the Great Bear Lake; also, he knew that in that direction the Arctic Circle cut its forbidding way across the Canadian Barrens. This stream in which he stood was a feeder to the Coppermine River, which in turn flowed north and emptied into Coronation Gulf and the Arctic Ocean. He had never been there, but he had seen it, once, on a Hudson Bay Company chart.

Again his gaze completed the circle of the world about him. It was not a heartening spectacle. Everywhere was soft skyline. The hills were all low-lying. There were no trees, no shrubs, no grasses—naught but a tremendous and terrible desolation that sent fear swiftly dawning into his eyes.

'Bill!' he whispered, once and twice; 'Bill!'

He cowered in the midst of the milky water, as though the vastness were pressing in upon him with overwhelming force, brutally crushing him with its complacent awfulness. He began to shake as with an ague-fit, till the gun fell from his hand with a splash. This served to rouse him. He fought with his fear and pulled himself together, groping in the water and recovering the weapon. He hitched his pack farther over on his left shoulder, so as to take a portion of its weight from off the injured ankle. Then he proceeded, slowly and carefully, wincing with pain, to the bank.

He did not stop. With a desperation that was madness, unmindful of the pain, he hurried up the slope to the crest of the hill over which his comrade had disappeared—more grotesque and comical by far than that limping, jerking comrade. But at the crest he saw a shallow valley, empty of life. He fought with his fear again, overcame it, hitched the pack still farther over on his left shoulder, and lurched on down the slope.

The bottom of the valley was soggy with water, which the thick moss held, spongelike, close to the surface. This water squirted out from under his feet at every step, and each time he lifted a foot the action culminated in a sucking sound as the wet moss reluctantly released its grip. He picked his way from muskeg to muskeg, and followed the other man's footsteps along and across the rocky ledges which thrust like islets through the sea of moss.

Though alone, he was not lost. Farther on he knew he would come to where dead spruce and fir, very small and weazened, bordered the shore of a little lake, the Titchin-nichilie, in the tongue of the country, the 'land of little sticks'. And into that lake flowed a small stream, the water of which was not milky. There was rush-grass on that stream—this he remembered well—but no timber, and he would follow it till its first trickle ceased at a divide. He would cross this divide to the first trickle of another stream, flowing to the west, which he would follow until it emptied into the river Dease, and here he would find a cache under an upturned canoe and piled over with many rocks. And in this cache would be ammunition for his empty gun, fish-hooks and lines, a small net—all the utilities for the killing and snaring of food. Also, he would find flour—not much—a piece of bacon, and some beans.

Bill would be waiting for him there, and they would paddle away south down the Dease to the Great Bear Lake. And south across the lake they would go, ever south, till they gained the Mackenzie. And south, still south, they would go, while the winter raced vainly after them, and the ice formed in the eddies, and the days grew chill and crisp, south to some warm Hudson Bay Company post, where timber grew tall and generous and there was grub without end.

These were the thoughts of the man as he strove onward. But hard as he strove with his body, he strove equally hard with his mind, trying to think that Bill had not deserted him, that Bill would surely wait for him at the cache. He was compelled to think this thought, or else there would not be any use to strive, and he would have lain down and died. And as the dim ball of the sun sank slowly into the northwest he covered every inch—and many times—of his and Bill's flight south before the downcoming winter. And he conned the grub of the cache and the grub of the Hudson Bay Company post over and over again. He had not eaten for two days; for a far longer time he had not had all he wanted to eat. Often he stooped and picked pale muskeg berries, put them into his mouth, and chewed and swallowed them. A muskeg berry is a bit of seed enclosed in a bit of water. In the mouth the water melts away and the seed chews sharp and bitter. The man knew there was no nourishment in the berries, but he chewed them patiently with a hope greater than knowledge and defying experience.

At nine o'clock he stubbed his toe on a rocky ledge, and from sheer weariness and weakness staggered and fell. He lay for some time, without movement, on his side. Then he slipped out of the pack-straps and clumsily dragged himself into a sitting posture. It was not yet dark, and in the lingering twilight he groped about among the rocks for shreds of dry moss. When he had gathered a heap he built a fire—a smouldering, smudgy fire—and put a tin pot of water on to boil.

He unwrapped his pack and the first thing he did was to count his matches. There were sixty-seven. He counted them three times to make sure. He divided them into several portions, wrapping them in oil paper, disposing of one bunch in his empty tobacco pouch, of another bunch in the inside band of his battered hat, of a third bunch under his shirt on the chest. This accomplished, a panic came upon him, and he unwrapped them all and counted them again. There were still sixty-seven.

He dried his wet footgear by the fire. The moccasins were in soggy shreds. The blanket socks were worn through in places, and his feet were raw and bleeding. His ankle was throbbing, and he gave it an examination. It had swollen to the size of his knee. He tore a long strip from one of his two blankets and bound the ankle tightly. He tore other strips and bound them about his feet to serve for both moccasins and socks. Then he drank the pot of water, steaming hot,wound his watch, and crawled between his blankets.

He slept like a dead man. The brief darkness around midnight came and went. The sun arose in the northeast—at least the day dawned in that quarter, for the sun was hidden by gray clouds.

At six o'clock he awoke, quietly lying on his back. He gazed straight up into the gray sky and knew that he was hungry. As he rolled over on his elbow he was startled by a loud snort, and saw a bull caribou regarding him with alert curiosity. The animal was not more than fifty feet away, and instantly into the man's mind leaped the vision and the savour of a caribou steak sizzling and frying over a fire. Mechanically he reached for the empty gun, drew a bead, and pulled the trigger. The bull snorted and leaped away, his hoofs rattling and clattering as he fled across the ledges.

The man cursed and flung the empty gun from him. He groaned aloud as he started to drag himself to his feet. It was a slow and arduous task. His joints were like rusty hinges. They worked harshly in their sockets, with much friction, and each bending or unbending was accomplished only through a sheer exertion of will. When he finally gained his feet, another minute or so was consumed in straightening up, so that he could stand erect as a man should stand.

He crawled up a small knoll and surveyed the prospect. There were no trees, no bushes, nothing but a gray sea of moss scarcely diversified by gray rocks, gray lakelets, and gray streamlets. The sky was gray. There was no sun nor hint of sun. He had no idea of north, and he had forgotten the way he had come to this spot the night before. But he was not lost. He knew that. Soon he would come to the land of the little sticks. He felt that it lay off to the left somewhere, not far—possibly just over the next low hill.

He went back to put his pack into shape for travelling. He assured himself of the existence of his three separate parcels of matches, though he did not stop to count them. But he did linger, debating, over a squat moose-hide sack. It was not large. He could hide it under his two hands. He knew that it weighed fifteen pounds—as much as all the rest of the pack—and it worried him. He finally set it to one side and proceeded to roll the pack. He paused to gaze at the squat moose-hide sack. He picked it up hastily with a defiant glance about him, as though the desolation were trying to rob him of it; and when he rose to his feet to stagger on into the day, it was included in the pack on his back.

He bore away to the left, stopping now and again to eat muskeg berries. His ankle had stiffened, his limp was more pronounced, but the pain of it was as nothing compared with the pain of his stomach. The hunger pangs were sharp. They gnawed and gnawed until he could not keep his mind steady on the course he must pursue to gain the land of little sticks. The muskeg berries did not allay this gnawing, while they made his tongue and the roof of his mouth sore with their irritating bite.

He came upon a valley where rock ptarmigan rose on whirring wings from the ledges and muskegs. Ker—ker—ker was the cry they made. He threw stones at them, but could not hit them. He placed his pack on the ground and stalked them as a cat stalks a sparrow. The sharp rocks cut through his pants' legs till his knees left a trail of blood; but the hurt was lost in the hurt of his hunger. He squirmed over the wet moss, saturating his clothes and chilling his body; but he was not aware of it, so great was his fever for food. And always the ptarmigan rose, whirring, before him, till their ker—ker—ker became a mock to him, and he cursed them and cried aloud at them with their own cry.

Once he crawled upon one that must have been asleep. He did not see it till it shot up in his face from its rocky nook. He made a clutch as startled as was the rise of the ptarmigan, and there remained in his hand three tail-feathers. As he watched its flight he hated it, as though it had done him some terrible wrong. Then he returned and shouldered his pack.

As the day wore along he came into valleys or swales where game was more plentiful. A band of caribou passed by, twenty and odd animals, tantalizingly within rifle range. He felt a wild desire to run after them, a certitude that he could run them down. A black fox came toward him, carrying a ptarmigan in his mouth. The man shouted. It was a fearful cry, but the fox, leaping away in fright, did not drop the ptarmigan.

Late in the afternoon he followed a stream, milky with lime, which ran through sparse patches of rush-grass. Grasping these rushes firmly near the root, he pulled up what resembled a young onion-sprout no larger than a shingle-nail. It was tender, and his teeth sank into it with a crunch that promised deliciously of food. But its fibres were tough. It was composed of stringy filaments saturated with water, like the berries, and devoid of nourishment. He threw off his pack and went into the rush-grass on hands and knees, crunching and munching, like some bovine creature.

He was very weary and often wished to rest—to lie down and sleep; but he was continually driven on—not so much by his desire to gain the land of little sticks as by his hunger. He searched little ponds for frogs and dug up the earth with his nails for worms, though he knew in spite that neither frogs nor worms existed so far north.

He looked into every pool of water vainly, until, as the long twilight came on, he discovered a solitary fish, the size of a minnow, in such a pool. He plunged his arm in up to the shoulder, but it eluded him. He reached for it with both hands and stirred up the milky mud at the bottom. In his excitement he fell in, wetting himself to the waist. Then the water was too muddy to admit of his seeing the fish, and he was compelled to wait until the sediment had settled.

The pursuit was renewed, till the water was again muddied. But he could not wait. He unstrapped the tin bucket and began to bale the pool. He baled wildly at first, splashing himself and flinging the water so short a distance that it ran back into the pool. He worked more carefully, striving to be cool, though his heart was pounding against his chest and his hands were trembling. At the end of half an hour the pool was nearly dry. Not a cupful of water remained. And there was no fish. He found a hidden crevice among the stones through which it had escaped to the adjoining and larger pool—a pool which he could not empty in a night and a day. Had he known of the crevice, he could have closed it with a rock at the beginning and the fish would have been his.

Thus he thought, and crumpled up and sank down upon the wet earth. At first he cried softly to himself, then he cried loudly to the pitiless desolation that ringed him around; and for a long time after he was shaken by great dry sobs.

He built a fire and warmed himself by drinking quarts of hot water, and made camp on a rocky ledge in the same fashion he had the night before. The last thing he did was to see that his matches were dry and to wind his watch. The blankets were wet and clammy. His ankle pulsed with pain. But he knew only that he was hungry, and through his restless sleep he dreamed of feasts and banquets and of food served and spread in all imaginable ways.

He awoke chilled and sick. There was no sun. The gray of earth and sky had become deeper, more profound. A raw wind was blowing, and the first flurries of snow were whitening the hilltops. The air about him thickened and grew white while he made a fire and boiled more water. It was wet snow, half rain, and the flakes were large and soggy. At first they melted as soon as they came in contact with the earth, but ever more fell, covering the ground, putting out the fire, spoiling his supply of moss-fuel.

This was a signal for him to strap on his pack and stumble onward, he knew not where. He was not concerned with the land of little sticks, nor with Bill and the cache under the upturned canoe by the river Dease. He was mastered by the verb 'to eat'.

He was hunger-mad. He took no heed of the course he pursued, so long as that course led him through the swale bottoms. He felt his way through the wet snow to the watery muskeg berries, and went by feel as he pulled up the rush-grass by the roots. But it was tasteless stuff and did not satisfy. He found a weed that tasted sour and he ate all he could find of it, which was not much, for it was a creeping growth, easily hidden under the several inches of snow.

He had no fire that night, nor hot water, and crawled under his blanket to sleep the broken hunger-sleep. The snow turned into a cold rain. He awakened many times to feel it falling on his upturned face. Day came—a gray day and no sun. It had ceased raining. The keenness of his hunger had departed. Sensibility, as far as concerned the yearning for food, had been exhausted. There was a dull, heavy ache in his stomach, but it did not bother him so much. He was more rational, and once more he was chiefly interested in the land of little sticks and the cache by the river Dease.

He ripped the remnant of one of his blankets into strips and bound his bleeding feet. Also, he recinched the injured ankle and prepared himself for a day of travel. When he came to his pack, he paused long over the squat moose-hide sack, but in the end it went with him.

The snow had melted under the rain, and only the hilltops showed white. The sun came out, and he succeeded in locating the points of the compass, though he knew now that he was lost. Perhaps, in his previous days' wanderings, he had edged away too far to the left. He now bore off to the right to counteract the possible deviation from his true course.

Though the hunger pangs were no longer so exquisite, he realized that he was weak. He was compelled to pause for frequent rests, when he attacked the muskeg berries and rush-grass patches. His tongue felt dry and large, as though covered with a fine hairy growth, and it tasted bitter in his mouth. His heart gave him a great deal of trouble. When he had travelled a few minutes it would begin a remorseless thump, thump, thump, and then leap up and away in a painful flutter of beats that choked him and made him go faint and dizzy.

In the middle of the day he found two minnows in a large pool. It was impossible to bale it, but he was calmer now and managed to catch them in his tin bucket. They were no longer than his little finger, but he was not particularly hungry. The dull ache in his stomach had been growing duller and fainter. It seemed almost that his stomach was dozing. He ate the fish raw, masticating with painstaking care, for the eating was an act of pure reason. While he had no desire to eat, he knew that he must eat to live.

In the evening he caught three more minnows, eating two and saving the third for breakfast. The sun had dried stray shreds of moss, and he was able to warm himself with hot water. He had not covered more than ten miles that day; and the next day, travelling whenever his heart permitted him, he covered no more than five miles. But his stomach did not give him the slightest uneasiness. It had gone to sleep. He was in a strange country, too, and the caribou were growing more plentiful, also the wolves. Often their yelps drifted across the desolation, and once he saw three of them slinking away before his path.

Another night; and in the morning, being more rational, he untied the leather string that fastened the squat moose-hide sack. From its open mouth poured a yellow stream of coarse gold-dust and nuggets. He roughly divided the gold in halves, caching one half on a prominent ledge, wrapped in a piece of blanket, and returning the other half to the sack. He also began to use strips of the one remaining blanket for his feet. He still clung to his gun, for there were cartridges in that cache by the river Dease.

This was a day of fog, and this day hunger awoke in him again. He was very weak and was afflicted with a giddiness which at times blinded him. It was no uncommon thing now for him to stumble and fall; and stumbling once, he fell squarely into a ptarmigan nest. There were four newly hatched chicks, a day old—little specks of pulsating life no more than a mouthful; and he ate them ravenously, thrusting them alive into his mouth and crunching them like egg-shells between his teeth. The mother ptarmigan beat about him with great outcry. He used his gun as a club with which to knock her over, but she dodged out of reach. He threw stones at her and with one chance shot broke a wing. Then she fluttered away, running, trailing the broken wing, with him in pursuit.

The little chicks had no more than whetted his appetite. He hopped and bobbed clumsily along on his injured ankle, throwing stones and screaming hoarsely at times; at other times hopping and bobbing silently along, picking himself up grimly and patiently when he fell, or rubbing his eyes with his hand when the giddiness threatened to overpower him.

The chase led him across swampy ground in the bottom of the valley, and he came upon footprints in the soggy moss. They were not his own—he could see that. They must be Bill's. But he could not stop, for the mother ptarmigan was running on. He would catch her first, then he would return and investigate. He exhausted the mother ptarmigan; but he exhausted himself. She lay panting on her side. He lay panting on his side, a dozen feet away, unable to crawl to her. And as he recovered she recovered, fluttering out of reach as his hungry hand went out to her. The chase was resumed. Night settled down and she escaped. He stumbled from weakness and pitched head foremost on his face, cutting his cheek, his pack upon his back. He did not move for a long while; then he rolled over on his side, wound his watch, and lay there until morning.

Another day of fog. Half of his last blanket had gone into foot-wrappings. He failed to pick up Bill's trail. It did not matter. His hunger was driving him too compellingly—only—only he wondered if Bill, too, were lost. By midday the irk of his pack became too oppressive. Again he divided the gold, this time merely spilling half of it on the ground. In the afternoon he threw the rest of it away, there remaining to him only the half-blanket, the tin bucket, and the rifle.

An hallucination began to trouble him. He felt confident that one cartridge remained to him. It was in the chamber of the rifle and he had overlooked it. On the other hand, he knew all the time that the chamber was empty. But the hallucination persisted. He fought it off for hours, then threw his rifle open and was confronted with emptiness. The disappointment was as bitter as though he had really expected to find the cartridge.

He plodded on for half an hour, when the hallucination arose again. Again he fought it, and still it persisted, till for very relief he opened his rifle to unconvince himself. At times his mind wandered farther afield, and he plodded on, a mere automaton, strange conceits and whimsicalities gnawing at his brain like worms. But these excursions out of the real were of brief duration, for ever the pangs of the hunger-bite called him back. He was jerked back abruptly once from such an excursion by a sight that caused him nearly to faint. He reeled and swayed, doddering like a drunken man to keep from falling. Before him stood a horse. A horse! He could not believe his eyes. A thick mist was in them, intershot with sparkling points of light. He rubbed his eyes savagely to clear his vision, and beheld, not a horse, but a great brown bear. The animal was studying him with bellicose curiosity.

The man had brought his gun halfway to his shoulder before he realized. He lowered it and drew his hunting-knife from its beaded sheath at his hip. Before him was meat and life. He ran his thumb along the edge of his knife. It was sharp. The point was sharp. He would fling himself upon the bear and kill it. But his heart began its warning thump, thump, thump. Then followed the wild upward leap and tattoo of flutters, the pressing as of an iron band about his forehead, the creeping of the dizziness into his brain.

His desperate courage was evicted by a great surge of fear. In his weakness, what if the animal attacked him? He drew himself up to his most imposing stature, gripping the knife and staring hard at the bear. The bear advanced clumsily a couple of steps, reared up, and gave vent to a tentative growl. If the man ran, he would run after him; but the man did not run. He was animated now with the courage of fear. He, too, growled, savagely, terribly, voicing the fear that is to life germane and that lies twisted about life's deepest roots.

The bear edged away to one side, growling menacingly, himself appalled by this mysterious creature that appeared upright and unafraid. But the man did not move. He stood like a statue till the danger was past, when he yielded to a fit of trembling and sank down into the wet moss.

He pulled himself together and went on, afraid now in a new way. It was not the fear that he should die passively from lack of food, but that he should be destroyed violently before starvation had exhausted the last particle of the endeavour in him that made toward surviving. There were the wolves. Back and forth across the desolation drifted their howls, weaving the very air into a fabric of menace that was so tangible that he found himself, arms in the air, pressing it back from him as it might be the walls of a wind-blown tent.

Now and again the wolves, in packs of two and three, crossed his path. But they steered clear of him. They were not in sufficient numbers, and besides they were hunting the caribou, which did not battle, while this strange creature that walked erect might scratch and bite.

In the late afternoon he came upon scattered bones where the wolves had made a kill. The debris had been a caribou calf an hour before, squawking and running and very much alive. He contemplated the bones, clean-picked and polished, pink with the cell-life in them which had not yet died. Could it possibly be that he might be that ere the day was done! Such was life, eh? A vain and fleeting thing. It was only life that pained. There was no hurt in death. To die was to sleep. It meant cessation, rest. Then why was he not content to die?

But he did not moralize long. He was squatting in the moss, a bone in his mouth, sucking at the shreds of life that still dyed it faintly pink. The sweet meaty taste, thin and elusive almost as a memory, maddened him. He closed his jaws on the bones and crunched. Sometimes it was the bone that broke, sometimes his teeth. Then he crushed the bones between rocks, pounded them to a pulp, and swallowed them. He pounded his fingers, too, in his haste, and yet found a moment in which to feel surprise at the fact that his fingers did not hurt much when caught under the descending rock.

Came frightful days of snow and rain. He did not know when he made camp, when he broke camp. He travelled in the night as much as in the day. He rested wherever he fell, crawled on whenever the dying life in him flickered up and burned less dimly. He, as a man, no longer strove. It was the life in him, unwilling to die, that drove him on. He did not suffer. His nerves had become blunted, numb, while his mind was filled with weird visions and delicious dreams.

But ever he sucked and chewed on the crushed bones of the caribou calf, the least remnants of which he had gathered up and carried with him. He crossed no more hills or divides, but automatically followed a large stream which flowed through a wide and shallow valley. He did not see this stream nor this valley. He saw nothing save visions. Soul and body walked or crawled side by side, yet apart, so slender was the thread that bound them.

He awoke in his right mind, lying on his back on a rocky ledge. The sun was shining bright and warm. Afar off he heard the squawking of caribou calves. He was aware of vague memories of rain and wind and snow, but whether he had been beaten by the storm for two days or two weeks he did not know.

For some time he lay without movement, the genial sunshine pouring upon him and saturating his miserable body with its warmth. A fine day, he thought. Perhaps he could manage to locate himself. By a painful effort he rolled over on his side. Below him flowed a wide and sluggish river. Its unfamiliarity puzzled him. Slowly he followed it with his eyes, winding in wide sweeps among the bleak, bare hills, bleaker and barer and lower-lying than any hills he had yet encountered. Slowly, deliberately, without excitement or more than the most casual interest, he followed the course of the strange stream toward the skyline and saw it emptying into a bright and shining sea. He was still unexcited. Most unusual, he thought, a vision or a mirage—more likely a vision, a trick of his disordered mind. He was confirmed in this by sight of a ship lying at anchor in the midst of the shining sea. He closed his eyes for a while, then opened them. Strange how the vision persisted! Yet not strange. He knew there were no seas or ships in the heart of the barren lands, just as he had known there was no cartridge in the empty rifle.

He heard a snuffle behind him—a half-choking gasp or cough. Very slowly, because of his exceeding weakness and stiffness, he rolled over on his other side. He could see nothing near at hand, but he waited patiently. Again came the snuffle and cough, and outlined between two jagged rocks not a score of feet away he made out the gray head of a wolf. The sharp ears were not pricked so sharply as he had seen them on other wolves; the eyes were bleared and bloodshot, the head seemed to droop limply and forlornly. The animal blinked continually in the sunshine. It seemed sick. As he looked it snuffled and coughed again.

This, at least, was real, he thought, and turned on the other side so that he might see the reality of the world which had been veiled from him before by the vision. But the sea still shone in the distance and the ship was plainly discernible. Was it reality, after all? He closed his eyes for a long while and thought, and then it came to him. He had been making north by east, away from the Dease Divide and into the Coppermine Valley. This wide and sluggish river was the Coppermine. That shining sea was the Arctic Ocean. That ship was a whaler, strayed east, far east, from the mouth of the Mackenzie, and it was lying at anchor in Coronation Gulf. He remembered the Hudson Bay Company chart he had seen long ago, and it was all clear and reasonable to him.

He sat up and turned his attention to immediate affairs. He had worn through the blanket-wrappings, and his feet were shapeless lumps of raw meat. His last blanket was gone. Rifle and knife were both missing. He had lost his hat somewhere, with the bunch of matches in the band, but the matches against his chest were safe and dry inside the tobacco pouch and oil paper. He looked at his watch. It marked eleven o'clock and was still running. Evidently he had kept it wound.

He was calm and collected. Though extremely weak, he had no sensation of pain. He was not hungry. The thought of food was not even pleasant to him, and whatever he did was done by his reason alone. He ripped off his pants' legs to the knees and bound them about his feet. Somehow he had succeeded in retaining the tin bucket. He would have some hot water before he began what he foresaw was to be a terrible journey to the ship.

His movements were slow. He shook as with a palsy. When he started to collect dry moss, he found he could not rise to his feet. He tried again and again, then contented himself with crawling about on hands and knees. Once he crawled near to the sick wolf. The animal dragged itself reluctantly out of his way, licking its chops with a tongue which seemed hardly to have the strength to curl. The man noticed that the tongue was not the customary healthy red. It was a yellowish brown and seemed coated with a rough and half-dry mucus.

After he had drunk a quart of hot water the man found he was able to stand, and even to walk as well as a dying man might be supposed to walk. Every minute or so he was compelled to rest. His steps were feeble and uncertain, just as the wolf's that trailed him were feeble and uncertain; and that night, when the shining sea was blotted out by blackness, he knew he was nearer to it by no more than four miles.

Throughout the night he heard the cough of the sick wolf, and now and then the squawking of the caribou calves. There was life all around him, but it was strong life, very much alive and well, and he knew the sick wolf clung to the sick man's trail in the hope that the man would die first. In the morning, on opening his eyes, he beheld it regarding him with a wistful and hungry stare. It stood crouched, with tail between its legs, like a miserable and woe-begone dog. It shivered in the chill morning wind, and grinned dispiritedly when the man spoke to it in a voice that achieved no more than a hoarse whisper.

The sun rose brightly, and all morning the man tottered and fell toward the ship on the shining sea. The weather was perfect. It was the brief Indian Summer of the high latitudes. It might last a week. Tomorrow or next day it might be gone.

In the afternoon the man came upon a trail. It was of another man, who did not walk, but who dragged himself on all fours. The man thought it might be Bill, but he thought in a dull, uninterested way. He had no curiosity. In fact, sensation and emotion had left him. He was no longer susceptible to pain. Stomach and nerves had gone to sleep. Yet the life that was in him drove him on. He was very weary, but it refused to die. It was because it refused to die that he still ate muskeg berries and minnows, drank his hot water, and kept a wary eye on the sick wolf.

He followed the trail of the other man who dragged himself along, and soon came to the end of it—a few fresh-picked bones where the soggy moss was marked by the footpads of many wolves. He saw a squat moose-hide sack, mate to his own, which had been torn by sharp teeth. He picked it up, though its weight was almost too much for his feeble fingers. Bill had carried it to the last. Ha! ha! He would have the laugh on Bill. He would survive and carry it to the ship in the shining sea. His mirth was hoarse and ghastly, like a raven's croak, and the sick wolf joined him, howling lugubriously. The man ceased suddenly. How could he have the laugh on Bill if that were Bill; if those bones, so inky-white and clean, were Bill?

He turned away. Well, Bill had deserted him; but he would not take the gold, nor would he suck Bill's bones. Bill would have, though, had it been the other way around, he mused as he staggered on. He came to a pool of water. Stooping over in quest of minnows, he jerked his head back as though he had been stung. He had caught sight of his reflected face. So horrible was it that sensibility awoke long enough to be shocked. There were three minnows in the pool, which was too large to drain; and after several ineffectual attempts to catch them in the tin bucket he forbore. He was afraid, because of his great weakness, that he might fall in and drown. It was for this reason that he did not trust himself to the river astride one of the many drift-logs which lined its sand-spits.

That day he decreased the distance between him and the ship by three miles; the next day by two—for he was crawling now as Bill had crawled; and the end of the fifth day found the ship still seven miles away and him unable to make even a mile a day. Still the Indian Summer held on, and he continued to crawl and faint, turn and turn about; and ever the sick wolf coughed and wheezed at his heels. His knees had become raw meat like his feet, and though he padded them with the shirt from his back it was a red track he left behind him on the moss and stones. Once, glancing back, he saw the wolf licking hungrily his bleeding trail, and he saw sharply what his own end might be—unless—unless he could get the wolf. Then began as grim a tragedy of existence as was ever played—a sick man that crawled, a sick wolf that limped, two creatures dragging their dying carcasses across the desolation and hunting each other's lives.

Had it been a well wolf, it would not have mattered so much to the man; but the thought of going to feed the maw of that loathsome and all but dead thing was repugnant to him. He was finicky. His mind had begun to wander again, and to be perplexed by hallucinations, while his lucid intervals grew rarer and shorter.

He was awakened once from a faint by a wheeze close in his ear. The wolf leaped lamely back, losing its footing and falling in its weakness. It was ludicrous, but he was not amused. Nor was he even afraid. He was too far gone for that. But his mind was for the moment clear, and he lay and considered. The ship was no more than four miles away. He could see it quite distinctly when he rubbed the mists out of his eyes, and he could see the white sail of a small boat cutting the water of the shining sea. But he could never crawl those four miles. He knew that, and was very calm in the knowledge. He knew that he could not crawl half a mile. And yet he wanted to live. It was unreasonable that he should die after all he had undergone. Fate asked too much of him. And, dying, he declined to die. It was stark madness, perhaps, but in the very grip of Death he defied Death and refused to die.

He closed his eyes and composed himself with infinite precaution. He steeled himself to keep above the suffocating languor that lapped like a rising tide through all the wells of his being. It was very like a sea, this deadly languor, that rose and rose and drowned his consciousness bit by bit. Sometimes he was all but submerged, swimming through oblivion with a faltering stroke; and again, by some strange alchemy of soul, he would find another shred of will and strike out more strongly.

Without movement he lay on his back, and he could hear, slowly drawing near and nearer, the wheezing intake and output of the sick wolf's breath. It drew closer, ever closer, through an infinitude of time, and he did not move. It was at his ear. The harsh dry tongue grated like sandpaper against his cheek. His hands shot out—or at least he willed them to shoot out. The fingers were curved like talons, but they closed on empty air. Swiftness and certitude require strength, and the man had not this strength.

The patience of the wolf was terrible. The man's patience was no less terrible. For half a day he lay motionless, fighting off unconsciousness and waiting for the thing that was to feed upon him and upon which he wished to feed. Sometimes the languid sea rose over him and he dreamed long dreams; but ever through it all, waking and dreaming, he waited for the wheezing breath and the harsh caress of the tongue.

He did not hear the breath, and he slipped slowly from some dream to the feel of the tongue along his hand. He waited. The fangs pressed softly; the pressure increased; the wolf was exerting its last strength in an effort to sink teeth in the food for which it had waited so long. But the man had waited long, and the lacerated hand closed on the jaw. Slowly, while the wolf struggled feebly and the hand clutched feebly, the other hand crept across to a grip. Five minutes later the whole weight of the man's body was on top of the wolf. The hands had not sufficient strength to choke the wolf, but the face of the man was pressed close to the throat of the wolf and the mouth of the man was full of hair. At the end of half an hour the man was aware of a warm trickle in his throat. It was not pleasant. It was like molten lead being forced into his stomach, and it was forced by his will alone. Later the man rolled over on his back and slept.

There were some members of a scientific expedition on the whale-ship *Bedford*. From the deck they remarked a strange object on the shore. It was moving down the beach toward the water. They were unable to classify it, and, being scientific men, they climbed into the whale-boat alongside and went ashore to see. And they saw something that was alive but which could hardly be called a man. It was blind, unconscious. It squirmed along the ground like some monstrous worm. Most of its efforts were ineffectual, but it was persistent, and it writhed and twisted and went ahead perhaps a score of feet an hour.

Three weeks afterward the man lay in a bunk on the whale-ship *Bedford*, and with tears streaming down his wasted cheeks told who he was and what he had undergone. He also babbled incoherently of his mother, of sunny Southern California, and a home among the orange groves and flowers.

The days were not many after that when he sat at table with the scientific men and ship's officers. He gloated over the spectacle of so much food, watching it anxiously as it went into the mouths of others. With the disappearance of each mouthful an expression of deep regret came into his eyes. He was quite sane, yet he hated those men at meal time. He was haunted by a fear that the food would not last. He inquired of the cook, the cabin-boy, the captain, concerning the food stores. They reassured him countless times; but he could not believe them, and pried cunningly about the lazarette to see with his own eyes.

It was noticed that the man was getting fat. He grew stouter with each day. The scientific men shook their heads and theorized. They limited the man at his meals, but still his girth increased and he swelled prodigiously under his shirt.

The sailors grinned. They knew. And when the scientific men set a watch on the man, they knew too. They saw him slouch for'ard after breakfast, and, like a mendicant, with outstretched palm, accost a sailor. The sailor grinned and passed him a fragment of sea biscuit. He clutched it avariciously, looked at it as a miser looks at gold, and thrust it into his shirt bosom. Similar were the donations from other grinning sailors.

The scientific men were discreet. They let him alone. But they privily examined his bunk. It was lined with hardtack; the mattress was stuffed with hardtack; every nook and cranny was filled with hardtack. Yet he was sane. He was taking precautions against another possible famine—that was all. He would recover from it, the scientific men said; and he did, ere the *Bedford's* anchor rumbled down in San Francisco Bay.

6

SMALL-BOAT SAILING

A sailor is born, not made. And by 'sailor' is meant, not the average efficient and hopeless creature who is found today in the forecastle of deepwater ships, but the man who will take a fabric compounded of wood and iron and rope and canvas and compel it to obey his will on the surface of the sea. Barring captains and mates of big ships, the small-boat sailor is the real sailor. He knows—he must know—how to make the wind carry his craft from one given point to another given point. He must know about tides and rips and eddies, bar and channel markings, and day and night signals; he must be wise in weather-lore; and he must be sympathetically familiar with the peculiar qualities of his boat which differentiate it from every other boat that was ever built and rigged. He must know how to gentle her about, as one instance of a myriad, and to fill her on the other tack without deadening her way or allowing her to fall off too far.

The deepwater sailor of today needs know none of these things. And he doesn't. He pulls and hauls as he is ordered, swabs decks, washes paint, and chips iron-rust. He knows nothing, and cares less. Put him in a small boat and he is helpless. He will cut an even better figure on the hurricane deck of a horse.

I shall never forget my child-astonishment when I first encountered one of these strange beings. He was a runaway

English sailor. I was a lad of twelve, with a decked-over, fourteen-foot, centre-board skiff which I had taught myself to sail. I sat at his feet as at the feet of a god, while he discoursed of strange lands and peoples, deeds of violence, and hair-raising gales at sea. Then, one day, I took him for a sail. With all the trepidation of the veriest little amateur, I hoisted sail and got under way. Here was a man, looking on critically, I was sure, who knew more in one second about boats and the water than I could ever know. After an interval, in which I exceeded myself, he took the tiller and the sheet. I sat on the little thwart amidships, open-mouthed, prepared to learn what real sailing was. My mouth remained open, for I learned what a real sailor was in a small boat. He couldn't trim the sheet to save himself, he nearly capsized several times in squalls, and, once again, by blunderingly jibing over; he didn't know what a centreboard was for, nor did he know that in running a boat before the wind one must sit in the middle instead of on the side; and finally, when we came back to the wharf, he ran the skiff in full tilt, shattering her nose and carrying away the mast-step. And yet he was a really truly sailor fresh from the vasty deep.

Which points my moral. A man can sail in the forecastles of big ships all his life and never know what real sailing is. From the time I was twelve, I listened to the lure of the sea. When I was fifteen I was captain and owner of an oyster-pirate sloop. By the time I was sixteen I was sailing in scow-schooners, fishing salmon with the Greeks up the Sacramento River, and serving as sailor on the Fish Patrol. And I was a good sailor, too, though all my cruising had been on San Francisco Bay and the rivers tributary to it. I had never been on the ocean in my life.

Then, the month I was seventeen, I signed before the mast as an able seaman on a three-top-mast schooner bound on a seven-months' cruise across the Pacific and back again. As my shipmates promptly informed me, I had had my nerve with me to sign on as able seaman. Yet behold, I was an able seaman. I had graduated from the right school. It took no more than minutes to learn the names and uses of the few new ropes. It was simple. I did not do things blindly. As a small-boat sailor I had learned to reason out and know the why of everything. It is true, I had to learn how to steer by compass, which took maybe half a minute; but when it came to steering 'full-and-by' and 'close-and-by', I could beat the average of my shipmates, because that was the very way I had always sailed. Inside fifteen minutes I could box the compass around and back again. And there was little else to learn during that seven-months' cruise, except fancy rope-sailorizing, such as the more complicated lanyard knots and the making of various kinds of sennit and rope-mats. The point of all of which is that it is by means of small-boat sailing that the real sailor is best schooled.

And if a man is a born sailor, and has gone to the school of the sea, never in all his life can he get away from the sea again. The salt of it is in his bones as well as his nostrils, and the sea will call to him until he dies. Of late years, I have found easier ways of earning a living. I have quit the forecastle for keeps, but always I come back to the sea. In my case it is usually San Francisco Bay, than which no lustier, tougher, sheet of water can be found for small-boat sailing.

It really blows on San Francisco Bay. During the winter, which is the best cruising season, we have southeasters, southwesters, and occasional howling northers. Throughout the summer we have what we call the 'sea-breeze', an unfailing wind off the Pacific that on most afternoons in the week blows what the Atlantic Coast yachtsmen would name a gale. They are always surprised by the small spread of canvas our yachts carry. Some of them, with schooners they have sailed around the Horn, have looked proudly at their own lofty sticks and huge spreads, then patronizingly and even pityingly at ours. Then, perchance, they have joined in a club cruise from San Francisco to Mare Island. They found the morning run up the Bay delightful. In the afternoon, when the brave west wind ramped across San Pablo Bay and they faced it on the long beat home, things were somewhat different. One by one, like a flight of swallows, our more meagrely sparred and canvassed yachts went by, leaving them wallowing and dead and shortening down in what they called a gale but which we called a dandy sailing breeze. The next time they came out, we would notice their sticks cut down, their booms shortened, and their after-leeches nearer the luffs by whole cloths.

As for excitement, there is all the difference in the world between a ship in trouble at sea, and a small boat in trouble on landlocked water. Yet for genuine excitement and thrill, give me the small boat. Things happen so quickly, and there are always so few to do the work—and hard work, too, as the small-boat sailor knows. I have toiled all night, both watches on deck, in a typhoon off the coast of Japan, and been less exhausted than by two hours' work at reefing down a thirty-foot sloop and heaving up two anchors on a lee shore in a screaming southeaster.

Hard work and excitement? Let the wind baffle and drop in a heavy tide-way just as you are sailing your little sloop through a narrow drawbridge. Behold your sails, upon which you are depending, flap with sudden emptiness, and then see the impish wind, with a haul of eight points, fill your jib aback with a gusty puff. Around she goes, and sweeps, not through the open draw, but broadside on against the solid piles. Hear the roar of the tide, sucking through the trestle. And hear and see your pretty, fresh-painted boat crash against the piles. Feel her stout little hull give to the impact. See the rail actually pinch in. Hear your canvas tearing, and see the black, square-ended timbers thrusting holes through it. Smash! There goes your topmast stay, and the topmast reels over drunkenly above you. There is a ripping and crunching. If it continues, your starboard shrouds will be torn out. Grab a rope—any rope—and take a turn around a pile. But the free end of the rope is too short. You can't make it fast, and you hold on and wildly yell for your one companion to get a turn with another and longer rope. Hold on! You hold on till you are purple in the face, till it seems your arms are dragging out of their sockets, till the blood bursts from the ends of your fingers. But you hold, and your partner gets the longer rope and makes it fast. You straighten up and look at your hands. They are ruined. You can scarcely relax the crooks of the fingers. The pain is sickening. But there is no time. The skiff, which is always perverse, is pounding against the barnacles on the piles which threaten to scrape its gunwale off. It's drop the peak! Down jib! Then you run lines, and pull and haul and heave, and exchange unpleasant remarks with the bridge-tender who is always willing to meet you more than half way in such repartee. And finally, at the end of an hour, with aching back, sweat-soaked shirt, and slaughtered hands, you are through and swinging along on the placid, beneficent tide between narrow banks where the cattle stand knee-deep and gaze wonderingly at you. Excitement! Work! Can you beat it in a calm day on the deep sea?

I've tried it both ways. I remember labouring in a fourteen days' gale off the coast of New Zealand. We were a tramp collier, rusty and battered, with six thousand tons of coal in our hold. Life lines were stretched fore and aft; and on our weather side, attached to smokestack guys and rigging, were huge rope-nettings, hung there for the purpose of breaking the force of the seas and so saving our mess-room doors. But the doors were smashed and the mess-rooms washed out just the same. And yet, out of it all, arose but the one feeling, namely, of monotony.

In contrast with the foregoing, about the liveliest eight days of my life were spent in a small boat on the west coast of Korea. Never mind why I was thus voyaging up the Yellow Sea during the month of February in below-zero weather. The point is that I was in an open boat, a sampan, on a rocky coast where there were no lighthouses and where the tides ran from thirty to sixty feet. My crew were Japanese fishermen. We did not speak each other's language. Yet there was nothing monotonous about that trip. Never shall I forget one particular cold bitter dawn, when, in the thick of driving snow, we took in sail and dropped our small anchor. The wind was howling out of the northwest, and we were on a lee shore. Ahead and astern, all escape was cut off by rocky headlands, against whose bases burst the unbroken seas. To windward a short distance, seen only between the snow-squalls, was a low rocky reef. It was this that inadequately protected us from the whole Yellow Sea that thundered in upon us.

The Japanese crawled under a communal rice mat and went to sleep. I joined them, and for several hours we dozed fitfully. Then a sea deluged us out with icy water, and we found several inches of snow on top of the mat. The reef to windward was disappearing under the rising tide, and moment by moment the seas broke more strongly over the rocks. The fishermen studied the shore anxiously. So did I, and with a sailor's eye, though I could see little chance for a swimmer to gain that surf-hammered line of rocks. I made signs toward the headlands on either flank. The Japanese shook their heads. I indicated that dreadful lee shore. Still they shook their heads and did nothing. My conclusion was that they were paralyzed by the hopelessness of the situation. Yet our extremity increased with every minute, for the rising tide was robbing us of the reef that served as buffer. It soon became a case of swamping at our anchor. Seas were splashing on board in growing volume, and we baled constantly. And still my fishermen crew eyed the surf-battered shore and did nothing.

At last, after many narrow escapes from complete swamping, the fishermen got into action. All hands tailed on to the anchor and hove it up. For'ard, as the boat's head paid off, we set a patch of sail about the size of a flour-sack. And we headed straight for shore. I unlaced my shoes, unbuttoned my great coat and coat, and was ready to make a quick partial strip a minute or so before we struck. But we didn't strike, and, as we rushed in, I saw the beauty of the situation. Before us opened a narrow channel, frilled at its mouth with breaking seas. Yet, long before, when I had scanned the shore closely, there had been no such channel. I *had forgotten the thirty-foot tide.* And it was for this tide that the Japanese had so precariously waited. We ran the frill of breakers, curved into a tiny sheltered bay where the water was scarcely flawed by the gale, and landed on a beach where the salt sea of the last tide lay frozen in long curving lines. And this was one gale of three in the course of those eight days in the sampan. Would it have been beaten on a ship? I fear me the ship would have gone aground on the outlying reef and that its people would have been incontinently and monotonously drowned.

There are enough surprises and mishaps in a three-days' cruise in a small boat to supply a great ship on the ocean for a full year. I remember, once, taking out on her trial trip a little thirty-footer I had just bought. In six days we had two stiff blows, and, in addition, one proper southwester and one rip-snorting southeaster. The slight intervals between these blows were dead calms. Also, in the six days, we were aground three times. Then, too, we tied up to the bank in the Sacramento River, and, grounding by an accident on the steep slope on a falling tide, nearly turned a side somersault down the bank. In a stark calm and heavy tide in the Carquinez Straits, where anchors skate on the channel-scoured bottom, we were sucked against a big dock and smashed and bumped down a quarter of a mile of its length before we could get clear. Two hours afterward, on San Pablo Bay, the wind was piping up and we were reefing down. It is no fun to pick up a skiff adrift in a heavy sea and gale. That was our next task, for our skiff, swamping, parted both towing painters we had bent on. Before we recovered it we had nearly killed ourselves with exhaustion, and we certainly had strained the sloop in every part from keelson to truck. And to cap it all, coming into our home port, beating up the narrowest part of the San Antonio Estuary, we had a shave of inches from collision with a big ship in tow of a tug. I have sailed the ocean in far larger craft a year at a time, in which period occurred no such chapter of moving incident.

After all, the mishaps are almost the best part of small-boat sailing. Looking back, they prove to be punctuations of joy. At the time they try your mettle and your vocabulary, and may make you so pessimistic as to believe that God has a grudge against you—but afterward, ah, afterward, with what pleasure you remember them and with what gusto do you relate them to your brother skippers in the fellowhood of small-boat sailing!

A narrow, winding slough; a half tide, exposing mud surfaced with gangrenous slime; the water itself filthy and discoloured by the waste from the vats of a nearby tannery; the marsh grass on either side mottled with all the shades of a decaying orchid; a crazy, ramshackled, ancient wharf; and at the end of the wharf a small, white-painted sloop. Nothing romantic about it. No hint of adventure. A splendid pictorial argument against the alleged joys of small-boat sailing. Possibly that is what Cloudesley and I thought, that sombre, leaden morning as we turned out to cook breakfast and wash decks. The latter was my stunt, but one look at the dirty water overside and another at my fresh-painted deck, deterred me. After breakfast, we started a game of chess. The tide continued to fall, and we felt the sloop begin to list. We played on until the chess men began to fall over. The list increased, and we went on deck. Bowline and stern-line were drawn taut. As we looked the boat listed still farther with an abrupt jerk. The lines were now very taut.

'As soon as her belly touches the bottom she will stop,' I said.

Cloudesley sounded with a boathook along the outside.

'Seven feet of water,' he announced. 'The bank is almost up and down. The first thing that touches will be her mast when she turns bottom up.'

An ominous, minute snapping noise came from the stern-line. Even as we looked, we saw a strand fray and part. Then we jumped. Scarcely had we bent another line between the stern and the wharf, when the original line parted. As we bent another line for'ard, the original one there crackled and parted. After that, it was an inferno of work and excitement.

We ran more and more lines, and more and more lines continued to part, and more and more the pretty boat went over on her side. We bent all our spare lines; we unrove sheets and halyards; we used our two-inch hawser; we fastened lines part way up the mast, half way up, and everywhere else. We toiled and sweated and enounced our mutual and sincere conviction that God's grudge still held against us. Country yokels came down on the wharf and sniggered at us. When Cloudesley let a coil of rope slip down the inclined deck into the vile slime and fished it out with seasick countenance, the yokels sniggered louder and it was all I could do to prevent him from climbing up on the wharf and committing murder.

By the time the sloop's deck was perpendicular, we had unbent the boom-lift from below, made it fast to the wharf, and, with the other end fast nearly to the masthead, heaved it taut with block and tackle. The lift was of steel wire. We were confident that it could stand the strain, but we doubted the holding-power of the stays that held the mast.

The tide had two more hours to ebb (and it was the big run-out), which meant that five hours must elapse ere the returning tide would give us a chance to learn whether or not the sloop would rise to it and right herself.

The bank was almost up and down, and at the bottom, directly beneath us, the fast-ebbing tide left a pit of the vilest, illest-smelling, illest-appearing muck to be seen in many a day's ride. Said Cloudesley to me gazing down into it:

'I love you as a brother. I'd fight for you. I'd face roaring lions, and sudden death by field and flood. But just the same, don't you fall into that.' He shuddered nauseously. 'For if you do, I haven't the grit to pull you out. I simply couldn't. You'd be awful. The best I could do would be to take a boathook and shove you down out of sight.'

We sat on the upper sidewall of the cabin, dangled our legs down the top of the cabin, leaned our backs against the deck, and played chess until the rising tide and the block and tackle on the boom-lift enabled us to get her on a respectable keel again. Years afterward, down in the South Seas, on the island of Ysabel, I was caught in a similar predicament. In order to clean her copper, I had careened the *Snark* broadside on to the beach and outward. When the tide rose, she refused to rise. The water crept in through the scuppers, mounted over the rail, and the level of the ocean slowly crawled up the slant of the deck. We battened down the engine-room hatch, and the sea rose to it and over it and climbed perilously near to the cabin companion way and skylight.

We were all sick with fever, but we turned out in the blazing tropic sun and toiled madly for several hours. We carried our heaviest lines ashore from our mast heads and heaved with our heaviest purchase until everything crackled including ourselves. We would spell off and lie down like dead men, then get up and heave and crackle again. And in the end, our lower rail five feet under water and the wavelets lapping the companion way combing, the sturdy little craft shivered and shook herself and pointed her masts once more to the zenith.

There is never lack of exercise in small-boat sailing, and the hard work is not only part of the fun of it, but it beats the doctors. San Francisco Bay is no mill pond. It is a large and draughty and variegated piece of water. I remember, one winter evening, trying to enter the mouth of the Sacramento. There was a freshet on the river, the flood tide from the bay had been beaten back into a strong ebb, and the lusty west wind died down with the sun. It was just sunset, and with a fair to middling breeze, dead aft, we stood still in the rapid current. We were squarely in the mouth of the river; but there was no anchorage and we drifted backward, faster and faster, and dropped anchor outside as the last breath of wind left us. The night came on, beautiful and warm and starry. My one companion cooked supper, while on deck I put everything in shape Bristol fashion. When we turned in at nine o'clock the weather-promise was excellent. (If I had carried a barometer I'd have known better.) By two in the morning our shrouds were thrumming in a piping breeze, and I got up and gave her more scope on her hawser. Inside another hour there was no doubt that we were in for a southeaster.

It is not nice to leave a warm bed and get out of a bad anchorage in a black blowy night, but we arose to the occasion, put in two reefs, and started to heave up. The winch was old, and the strain of the jumping head sea was too much for it. With the winch out of commission, it was impossible to heave up by hand. We knew, because we tried it and slaughtered our hands. Now a sailor hates to lose an anchor. It is a matter of pride. Of course, we could have buoyed ours and slipped it. Instead, however, I gave her still more hawser, veered her, and dropped the second anchor.

There was little sleep after that, for first one and then the other of us would be rolled out of our bunks. The increasing size of the seas told us we were dragging, and when we struck the scoured channel we could tell by the feel of it that our two anchors were fairly skating across. It was a deep channel, the farther edge of it rising steeply like the wall of a canyon, and when our anchors started up that wall they hit in and held.

Yet, when we fetched up, through the darkness we could hear the seas breaking on the solid shore astern, and so near was it that we shortened the skiff's painter.

Daylight showed us that between the stern of the skiff and destruction was no more than a score of feet. And how it did blow! There were times, in the gusts, when the wind must have approached a velocity of seventy or eighty miles an hour. But the anchors held, and so nobly that our final anxiety was that the for'ard bitts would be jerked clean out of the boat. All day the sloop alternately ducked her nose under and sat down on her stern; and it was not till late afternoon that the storm broke in one last and worst mad gust. For a full five minutes an absolute dead calm prevailed, and then, with the suddenness of a thunderclap, the wind snorted out of the southwest—a shift of eight points and a boisterous gale. Another night of it was too much for us, and we hove up by hand in a cross head-sea. It was not stiff work. It was heartbreaking. And I know we were both near to crying from the hurt and the exhaustion. And when we did get the first anchor up-and-down we couldn't break it out. Between seas we snubbed her nose down to it, took plenty of turns, and stood clear as she jumped. Almost everything smashed and parted except the anchor-hold. The chocks were jerked out, the rail torn off, and the very covering-board splintered, and still the anchor held. At last, hoisting the reefed mainsail and slacking off a few of the hard-won feet of the chain, we sailed the anchor out. It was nip and tuck, though, and there were times when the boat was knocked down flat. We repeated the manoeuvre with the remaining anchor, and in the gathering darkness fled into the shelter of the river's mouth.

I was born so long ago that I grew up before the era of gasolene. As a result, I am old-fashioned. I prefer a sail boat to a motor boat, and it is my belief that boat-sailing is a finer, more difficult, and sturdier art than running a motor. Gasolene engines are becoming fool proof, and while it is unfair to say that any fool can run an engine, it is fair to say that almost any one can. Not so, when it comes to sailing a boat. More skill, more intelligence, and a vast deal more training are necessary. It is the finest training in the world for boy and youth and man. If the boy is very small, equip him with a small, comfortable skiff. He will do the rest.

He won't need to be taught. Shortly he will be setting a tiny leg-of-mutton and steering with an oar. Then he will begin to talk keels and centreboards and want to take his blankets out and stop aboard all night.

But don't be afraid for him. He is bound to run risks and encounter accidents. Remember, there are accidents in the nursery as well as out on the water. More boys have died from hot house culture than have died on boats large and small; and more boys have been made into strong and reliant men by boat-sailing than by lawn-croquet and dancing-school.

And once a sailor, always a sailor. The savour of the salt never stales. The sailor never grows so old that he does not care to go back for one more wrestling bout with wind and wave. I know it of myself. I have turned rancher, and live beyond sight of the sea. Yet I can stay away from it only so long. After several months have passed, I begin to grow restless. I find myself day dreaming over incidents of the last cruise, or wondering if the striped bass are running on Wingo Slough, or eagerly reading the newspapers for reports of the first northern flights of ducks. And then, suddenly, there is a hurried pack of suitcases and overhauling of gear, and we are off for Vallejo where the little *Roamer* lies, waiting, always waiting, for the skiff to come alongside, for the lighting of the fire in the galley-stove, for the pulling off of gaskets, the swinging up of the mainsail, and the rat-tat-tat of the reef-points, for the heaving short and the breaking out, and for the twirling of the wheel as she fills away and heads up Bay or down.

7

THE HANDSOME CABIN BOY

'AND the dapper young fellow was—'

'None other than the veiled woman, of course.'

'O, pshaw!' I cried. 'That's well enough for a Sunday newspaper, but in real life people are not so easily misled.'

'Look at the authentic instances—women serving as soldiers, sailors, scouts—'

'Bosh!'

'Why, there's my little brother Bob, as clever an impersonator—'

'Bosh!'

'People are fooled every day and—'

'Stuff and nonsense,' I said. 'Anyone but a ninny should penetrate such a make-up at a glance. I don't think much of a fellow who can't tell a man from a woman. Catch me napping that way.'

'I'll catch you,' cried Jack.

'I like that,' was my reply.

'I'll wager I fool you within six months.'

'Done! For how much?'

'The loser to foot a supper; the setting, ordering, and inviting of the same to be at the winner's discretion.'

'Done!'

We shook hands, and the fellows crowded round with all

sorts of advice and persiflage. Thus was the seed sown, out of which was to spring the never-to-be-forgotten romance of 'The Handsome Cabin Boy'.

The succeeding fortnight found me in solitary grandeur aboard my schooner yacht *Falcon*, bound for a short cruise to Honolulu. We had hardly sunk the Farralone Light, when my suspicions were aroused. From the cook to the sailing-master complaints began to pour in about the new cabin boy. They held he was willing enough, but worthless. At the last moment, Billy, the old boy, had left us in the lurch, and my agent, to whom all such matters were entrusted, had hastily procured the present incumbent.

As they said, he was willing enough, but—in short, he was ignorant of his duties and totally unfit for such a position. Yet he tried so hard that everybody was drawn toward him. And he was such a handsome lad. Dark-eyed, rosy-cheeked, with a delicate olive complexion and an exquisite oval—small wonder that he recalled to my mind the bet with Jack Haliday. And then, for the slender lad of fifteen or sixteen that he appeared, there was a vague, insinuating fullness about the figure, which did not fail to corroborate my suspicions.

But I held my hush and awaited confirmation. This came sooner than I expected. The sailing-master and myself were on the poop, one noon, with our sextants, bent on shooting the sun. The lad came up the companionway with a pan of soot and ashes; he had just cleaned the cabin stove. Instead of going to the lee, he stepped to the weather rail and let fly the refuse. And fly it did—backwards, of course, and all over us.

Digging a handful out of his eyes, the sailing-master grabbed the young rascal by the arm. Now Nelson was a rough son of the sea, and had a mellifluous command of the vernacular which serves for emphasis to those who sail the same. He shook him up and down and cursed him with as virile a combination of English and Scandinavian oaths as was ever my luck to hear.

The boy lost his wits and began to cry. Picking up the pan, he started for the cabin, but just opposite me, reeled and toppled over. I caught him before he could fall, and—well, my arm had strayed in forbidden pastures too often to be mistaken now.

'Why, you're a girl!' I cried.

The man at the wheel began to snicker, so I hurried her below to save her from confusion before the men. There she cried, and sobbed, and carried on, till I was almost as distracted myself, in my efforts to soothe her. At last she calmed down.

'O, sir,' she began, 'I hope you won't be angry with me. I—he—Mr—'

'It's Jack Haliday's doing, isn't it?' I interrupted.

'Yes, sir.'

'Then you know all about the bet, and you'll have to testify that I discovered your—er—identity.'

'Yes, sir, and he'll be angry because I lost. Boo—hoo—oo—'

'O, you did very well.' I thought she needed a little cheering. 'The cook would never have discovered—say! how the deuce—you'll have to change your—'

It was indeed embarrassing for both of us. And that blundering cook had never tumbled! I called him into the cabin.

'Tell off that German deck boy to help you,' I ordered. 'And go to your room and pack up Miss—er—'

'E—E—Eastman,' sobbed the disconsolate bundle on the floor.

'And pack up Miss Eastman's belongings. Take them to the spare state-room, and make everything comfortable. I'll see you get extra pay for this trip. Go! Don't stand there all day!' I could not help laughing at his round-eyed wonder.

'I don't know what to do in the way of suitable clothes,' I said, as she entered her new berth in the wake of a trim little sea-chest.

'That's all right, sir,' she replied, between her sobs. 'I b—brought some dresses along.'

'Strike me blind!' cried the cook, as the door shut. 'O, I beg your pardon, sir; but do you mean to tell me, sir, that he's a—a she? Think of it!—and me a married man! What'll my wife say?'

Though I tried to explain that there was no necessity of his wife knowing, he wandered away to the galley, more woe-begone, if anything, than the poor creature who had caused his distress. Still, I could sympathize with him, realizing as I did, my own false position, and knowing how the sailors must be haw-hawing among themselves.

Dinner was sent into her, and it was not till next morning that she showed herself. And then it was a demure little maid, for all her short brown locks. It seemed a pity they had been clipped for the sake of a paltry bet.

'What will your people say?' I asked, in the course of explanations. 'Do they know?'

'My brother does. I came with his consent.'

'Your brother's a scoundrel and ought to be horse whipped. It's disgraceful, to say the least.'

'How?'

This was a poser. How? I began to comprehend the mess Jack Haliday had got me into. How? What innocence!

'You must have been brought up in a convent,' I said bluntly.

'Yes, sir; I went to the Sacred Heart until a year ago.'

Worse and worse—it was no light responsibility thus thrust upon me. I finally wormed her story from her. She had lost her mother during her childhood, and her father, a small tradesman, had educated her at the Convent of the Sacred Heart. Things had gone from bad to worse with him, and when he died, she and her brother were left penniless. To curtail the story: they had become protégés of Haliday's. She had shown an aptitude for the stage, and Haliday encouraged her, prophesying that some day the metropolitan vaudeville would open its arms to a soubrette of no mean ability.

'And when he asked this favour of me,' she concluded, 'what

could I do? Refuse, after all he had done for me?'

Well, the yacht took on new life. Strange how this chit of a child, this girl of sixteen, brightened things up! She became the idol of all hands and even Nelson apologized—first time the stubborn dog ever did such a thing, I'll wager. She could play the piano fairly well, and though her voice was not strong and had no register, her singing was sweet indeed.

When we arrived at Honolulu, I was for making arrangements to send her back by steamer; but the guiless creature would not hear of it, and looked so miserable when I insisted, that I gave in. Besides, nobody knew us. And she—why, she had no conception of evil, and to undeceive her was a task beyond my power. I supplied her with funds, and she soon had a stunning array of gowns and other female fripperies. Then we took in the concerts of the Hawaiian Band, made long drives into the country, and visited many places of interest and recreation. We had a delightful time; but the best of good things must end, and a month later found us off the Golden Gate. Tomorrow we should be in San Francisco.

Tomorrow—I half sighed as I lighted a cigar, and glanced at her state-room door. What were her dreams, I wondered. Then I thought of my long, lonely cruises. How bright this one had been! Life took on new possibilities, as I began to realize some of its hitherto unknown charms—charms which my benedict friends never ceased to dwell upon. How she had changed things! A neatly turned ankle on the cabin stairs, a twinkling slipper along the deck, a girl's light laughter, a song at twilight, a—in short, the ineffable something of a woman's presence. I was startled at the thought. Let me see: sixteen—twenty-six; nineteen—twenty-nine; no, that would be too long to wait, eighteen—twenty-eight—that's it. And not such a disparity after all. Two years! What would not two years do? Development, the rounding of that mind—aye, and that form, already so rich of promise. Two years, and then—

'Eight bells!'

The clamour of changing watch had destroyed the fairy pictures; so I tossed away my cigar and went to bed.

Jack Haliday and the whole crowd were at the clubhouse pier to meet us. Evidently, the lookout of the Merchants' Exchange had telegraphed our arrival off the Heads the previous night. They trooped aboard in a body, and I trembled for Miss Eastman. However, Clara, as I had come to call her, faced the ordeal bravely. The subdued expectancy and smothered giggles angered me. Jack Haliday opened the ball at once.

'I say, you know, about that supper—'

'What about it?' I asked sharply.

'Well, I've made all the plans, but I thought it better to submit them to you. You might make a few suggestions, you know.'

'You've made all the plans!' I shouted. 'I have an idea that the ordering of this supper belongs to me.'

'Ha! ha! ha!' Everybody began to laugh.

'Hope you had a pleasant trip, Miss Eastman,' he said, turning to her.

'O, I did,' she assured him, though I could see her lips were trembling.

'How did you discover it?' he asked, addressing me.

'Why she fainted in my arms, and—'

'Ho! Ho! He! He! He!' the crowd fairly roared, and I beamed triumphantly on my discomfited opponent.

'Was he angry?' continued the imperturbable Haliday.

'No,' Clara replied, 'he was real nice. And when we got to Honolulu he wanted to send me home on the steamer, but I wouldn't let him. Then we had a gorgeous time—bought me candy and gloves, took me buggy riding, and—'

With this the crowd went mad. They slapped Jack on the shoulder, poked him in the ribs, and hugged each other in ecstasies of glee.

'Why, you ninny!' Jack cried. 'That's my brother Bob.'

'Impossible,' I rejoined. 'Why, when she fainted in my arms, I—'

At this juncture speech failed me, for the modest Miss Eastman turned a couple of backflips, came up smiling, thrust a hand into her maidenly bosom and drew forth—heavens!—a couple of pneumatic cushions, the kind used by football players.

It were needless for me to tell how I led the stampede to the clubhouse; how the supper came off, with Bob Haliday at the head of the table; or how, to this day, the mere mention of 'The Handsome Cabin Boy' arouses a certain choler which I can never hope to overcome.

8

THE LAW OF LIFE

Old Koskoosh listened greedily. Though his sight had long since faded, his hearing was still acute, and the slightest sound penetrated to the glimmering intelligence which yet abode behind the withered forehead, but which no longer gazed forth upon the things of the world. Ah! that was Sit-cum-to-ha, shrilly anathematizing the dogs as she cuffed and beat them into the harnesses. Sit-cum-to-ha was his daughter's daughter, but she was too busy to waste a thought upon her broken grandfather, sitting alone there in the snow, forlorn and helpless. Camp must be broken. The long trail waited while the short day refused to linger. Life called her, and the duties of life, not death. And he was very close to death now.

The thought made the old man panicky for the moment, and he stretched forth a palsied hand which wandered tremblingly over the small heap of dry wood beside him. Reassured that it was indeed there, his hand returned to the shelter of his mangy furs, and he again fell to listening. The sulky crackling of half-frozen hides told him that the chief's moose-skin lodge had been struck, and even then was being rammed and jammed into portable compass. The chief was his son, stalwart and strong, headman of the tribesmen, and a mighty hunter. As the women toiled with the camp luggage, his voice rose, chiding them for their slowness. Old

Koskoosh strained his ears. It was the last time he would hear that voice. There went Geehow's lodge! And Tusken's! Seven, eight, nine; only the shaman's could be still standing. There! They were at work upon it now. He could hear the shaman grunt as he piled it on the sled. A child whimpered, and a woman soothed it with soft, crooning gutturals. Little Koo-tee, the old man thought, a fretful child, and not overstrong. It would die soon, perhaps, and they would burn a hole through the frozen tundra and pile rocks above to keep the wolverines away. Well, what did it matter? A few years at best, and as many an empty belly as a full one. And in the end, Death waited, ever-hungry and hungriest of them all.

What was that? Oh, the men lashing the sleds and drawing tight the thongs. He listened, who would listen no more. The whiplashes snarled and bit among the dogs. Hear them whine! How they hated the work and the trail! They were off! Sled after sled churned slowly away into the silence. They were gone. They had passed out of his life, and he faced the last bitter hour alone. No. The snow crunched beneath a moccasin; a man stood beside him; upon his head a hand rested gently. His son was good to do this thing. He remembered other old men whose sons had not waited after the tribe. But his son had. He wandered away into the past, till the young man's voice brought him back.

'Is it well with you?' he asked.

And the old man answered, 'It is well.'

'There be wood beside you,' the younger man continued, 'and the fire burns bright. The morning is gray, and the cold has broken. It will snow presently. Even now is it snowing.'

'My voice is become like an old woman's.'

'Ay, even now is it snowing.'

'The tribesmen hurry. Their bales are heavy, and their bellies flat with lack of feasting. The trail is long and they travel fast. Go now. It is well?'

'It is well. I am as a last year's leaf, clinging lightly to the stem.

The first breath that blows, and I fall. My voice is become like an old woman's. My eyes no longer show me the way of my feet, and my feet are heavy, and I am tired. It is well.'

He bowed his head in content till the last noise of the complaining snow had died away, and he knew his son was beyond recall. Then his hand crept out in haste to the wood. It alone stood between him and the eternity that yawned in upon him. At last the measure of his life was a handful of faggots. One by one they would go to feed the fire, and just so, step by step, death would creep upon him. When the last stick had surrendered up its heat, the frost would begin to gather strength. First his feet would yield, then his hands; and the numbness would travel, slowly, from the extremities to the body. His head would fall forward upon his knees, and he would rest. It was easy. All men must die.

He did not complain. It was the way of life, and it was just. He had been born close to the earth, close to the earth had he lived, and the law thereof was not new to him. It was the law of all flesh. Nature was not kindly to the flesh. She had no concern for that concrete thing called the individual. Her interest lay in the species, the race. This was the deepest abstraction old Koskoosh's barbaric mind was capable of, but he grasped it firmly. He saw it exemplified in all life. The rise of the sap, the bursting greenness of the willow bud, the fall of the yellow leaf—in this alone was told the whole history. But one task did Nature set the individual. Did he not perform it, he died. Did he perform it, it was all the same, he died. Nature did not care; there were plenty who were obedient, and it was only the obedience in this matter, not the obedient, which lived and lived always. The tribe of Koskoosh was very old. The old men he had known when a boy, had known old men before them. Therefore it was true that the tribe lived, that it stood for the obedience of all its members, way down into the forgotten past, whose very resting places were unremembered. They did not count; they were episodes. They had passed away like clouds from a summer sky. He also was an episode, and would pass away. Nature did not care. To life she set one task, gave one law. To perpetuate was the task of life, its law was death. A maiden was a good creature to look upon, full-breasted and strong, with spring to her step and light in her eyes. But her task was yet before her. The light in her eyes brightened, her step quickened, she was now bold with the young men, now timid, and she gave them of her own unrest. And ever she grew fairer and yet fairer to look upon, till some hunter, able no longer to withhold himself, took her to his lodge to cook and toil for him and to become the mother of his children. And with the coming of her offspring her looks left her. Her limbs dragged and shuffled, her eyes dimmed and bleared, and only the little children found joy against the withered cheek of the old squaw by the fire. Her task was done. But a little while, on the first pinch of famine or the first long trail, and she would be left, even as he had been left, in the snow, with a little pile of wood. Such was the law.

He placed a stick carefully upon the fire and resumed his meditations. It was the same everywhere, with all things. The mosquitoes vanished with the first frost. The little tree-squirrel crawled away to die. When age settled upon the rabbit it became slow and heavy, and could no longer outfoot its enemies. Even the big bald-face grew clumsy and blind and quarrelsome, in the end to be dragged down by a handful of yelping huskies. He remembered how he had abandoned his own father on an upper reach of the Klondike one winter, the winter before the missionary came with his talk-books and his box of medicines. Many a time had Koskoosh smacked his lips over the recollection of that box, though now his mouth refused to moisten. The 'painkiller' had been especially good. But the missionary was a bother after all, for he brought no meat into the camp, and he ate heartily, and the hunters grumbled. But he chilled his lungs on the divide by the Mayo, and the dogs afterwards nosed the stones away and fought over his bones.

Koskoosh placed another stick on the fire and harked back deeper into the past. There was the time of the Great Famine, when the old men crouched empty-bellied to the fire, and let fall from their lips dim traditions of the ancient day when the Yukon ran wide open for three winters, and then lay frozen for three summers. He had lost his mother in that famine. In the summer the salmon run had failed, and the tribe looked forward to the winter and the coming of the caribou. Then the winter came, but with it there were no caribou. Never had the like been known, not even in the lives of the old men. But the caribou did not come, and it was the seventh year, and the rabbits had not replenished, and the dogs were naught but bundles of bones. And through the long darkness the children wailed and died, and the women, and the old men; and not one in ten of the tribe lived to meet the sun when it came back in the spring. That *was* a famine!

But he had seen times of plenty, too, when the meat spoiled on their hands, and the dogs were fat and worthless with overeating—times when they let the game go unkilled, and the women were fertile, and the lodges were cluttered with sprawling men-children and women-children. Then it was the men became high-stomached, and revived ancient quarrels, and crossed the divides to the south to kill the Pellys, and to the west that they might sit by the dead fires of the Tananas. He remembered, when a boy, during a time of plenty, when he saw a moose pulled down by the wolves. Zing-ha lay with him in the snow and watched—Zing-ha, who later became the craftiest of hunters, and who, in the end, fell through an air-hole on the Yukon. They found him, a month afterward, just as he had crawled halfway out and frozen stiff to the ice.

But the moose. Zing-ha and he had gone out that day to play at hunting after the manner of their fathers. On the bed of the creek they struck the fresh track of a moose, and with it the tracks of many wolves. 'An old one,' Zing-ha, who was quicker at reading the sign, said—'an old one who cannot keep up with the herd. The wolves have cut him out from his brothers, and they will never leave him.' And it was so. It was their way. By day and by night, never resting, snarling on his heels, snapping at his nose, they would stay by him to the end. How Zing-ha and he felt the bloodlust quicken! The finish would be a sight to see!

Eager-footed, they took the trail, and even he, Koskoosh, slow of sight and an unversed tracker, could have followed it blind, it was so wide. Hot were they on the heels of the chase, reading the grim tragedy, fresh-written, at every step. Now they came to where the moose had made a stand. Thrice the length of a grown man's body, in every direction, had the snow been stamped about and uptossed. In the midst were the deep impressions of the splay-hoofed game, and all about, everywhere, were the lighter footmarks of the wolves. Some, while their brothers harried the kill, had lain to one side and rested. The full-stretched impress of their bodies in the snow was as perfect as though made the moment before. One wolf had been caught in a wild lunge of the maddened victim and trampled to death. A few bones, well picked, bore witness.

Again, they ceased the uplift of their snowshoes at a second stand. Here the great animal had fought desperately. Twice had he been dragged down, as the snow attested, and twice had he shaken his assailants clear and gained footing once more. He had done his task long since, but none the less was life dear to him. Zing-ha said it was a strange thing, a moose once down to get free again; but this one certainly had. The shaman would see signs and wonders in this when they told him.

And yet again, they come to where the moose had made to mount the bank and gain the timber. But his foes had laid on from behind, till he reared and fell back upon them, crushing two deep into the snow. It was plain the kill was at hand, for their brothers had left them untouched. Two more stands were hurried past, brief in time-length and very close together. The trail was red now, and the clean stride of the great beast had grown short and slovenly. Then they heard the first sounds of the battle—not the full-throated chorus of the chase, but the short, snappy bark which spoke of close quarters and teeth to flesh. Crawling up the wind, Zing-ha bellied it through the snow, and with him crept he, Koskoosh, who was to be chief of the tribesmen in the years to come. Together they shoved aside the under-branches of a young spruce and peered forth. It was the end they saw.

The picture, like all of youth's impressions, was still strong with him, and his dim eyes watched the end played out as vividly as in that far-off time. Koskoosh marvelled at this, for in the days which followed, when he was a leader of men and a head of councillors, he had done great deeds and made his name a curse in the mouths of the Pellys, to say naught of the strange white man he had killed, knife to knife, in open fight.

For long he pondered on the days of his youth, till the fire died down and the frost bit deeper. He replenished it with two sticks this time, and gauged his grip on life by what remained. If Sit-cum-to-ha had only remembered her grandfather, and gathered a larger armful, his hours would have been longer. It would have been easy. But she was ever a careless child, and honoured not her ancestors from the time the Beaver, son of the son of Zing-ha, first cast eyes upon her. Well, what mattered it? Had he not done likewise in his own quick youth? For a while he listened to the silence. Perhaps the heart of his son might soften, and he would come back with the dogs to take his old father on with the tribe to where the caribou ran thick and the fat hung heavy upon them.

He strained his ears, his restless brain for the moment stilled. Not a stir, nothing. He alone took breath in the midst of the great silence. It was very lonely. Hark! What was that? A chill passed over his body. The familiar, long-drawn howl broke the void, and it was close at hand. Then on his darkened eyes was projected the vision of the moose—the old bull moose—the torn flanks and bloody sides, the riddled mane, and the great branching horns, down low and tossing to the last. He saw the flashing forms of gray, the gleaming eyes, the lolling tongues, the slavered fangs. And he saw the inexorable circle close in till it became a dark point in the midst of the stamped snow.

A cold muzzle thrust against his cheek, and at its touch his soul leaped back to the present. His hand shot into the fire and dragged out a burning faggot. Overcome for the nonce by his hereditary fear of man, the brute retreated, raising a prolonged call to his brothers; and greedily they answered, till a ring of crouching, jaw-slobbered gray was stretched round about. The old man listened to the drawing in of this circle. He waved his brand wildly, and sniffs turned to snarls; but the panting brutes refused to scatter. Now one wormed his chest forward, dragging his haunches after, now a second, now a third; but never a one drew back. Why should he cling to life? he asked, and dropped the blazing stick into the snow. It sizzled and went out. The circle grunted uneasily, but held its own. Again he saw the last stand of the old bull moose, and Koskoosh dropped his head wearily upon his knees. What did it matter after all? Was it not the law of life?

9

THE PEN

For two days I toiled in the prison-yard. It was heavy work, and, in spite of the fact that I malingered at every opportunity, I was played out. This was because of the food. No man could work hard on such food. Bread and water, that was all that was given us. Once a week we were supposed to get meat; but this meat did not always go around, and since all nutriment had first been boiled out of it in the making of soup, it didn't matter whether one got a taste of it once a week or not.

Furthermore, there was one vital defect in the bread-and-water diet. While we got plenty of water, we did not get enough of the bread. A ration of bread was about the size of one's two fists, and three rations a day were given to each prisoner. There was one good thing, I must say, about the water—it was hot. In the morning it was called 'coffee', at noon it was dignified as 'soup', and at night it masqueraded as 'tea'. But it was the same old water all the time. The prisoners called it 'water bewitched'. In the morning it was black water, the colour being due to boiling it with burnt bread-crusts. At noon it was served minus the colour, with salt and a drop of grease added. At night it was served with a purplish-auburn hue that defied all speculation; it was darn poor tea, but it was dandy hot water.

We were a hungry lot in the Erie County Pen. Only the

'long-timers' knew what it was to have enough to eat. The reason for this was that they would have died after a time on the fare we 'short-timers' received. I know that the long-timers got more substantial grub, because there was a whole row of them on the ground floor in our hall, and when I was a trusty, I used to steal from their grub while serving them. Man cannot live on bread alone and not enough of it.

My pal delivered the goods. After two days of work in the yard I was taken out of my cell and made a trusty, a 'hall-man'. At morning and night we served the bread to the prisoners in their cells; but at twelve o'clock a different method was used. The convicts marched in from work in a long line. As they entered the door of our ball, they broke the lock-step and took their hands down from the shoulders of their line-mates. Just inside the door were piled trays of bread, and here also stood the First Hall-man and two ordinary hall-men. I was one of the two. Our task was to hold the trays of bread as the line of convicts filed past. As soon as the tray, say, that I was holding was emptied, the other hall-man took my place with a full tray. And when his was emptied, I took his place with a full tray. Thus the line tramped steadily by, each man reaching with his right hand and taking one ration of bread from the extended tray.

The task of the First Hall-man was different. He used a club. He stood beside the tray and watched. The hungry wretches could never get over the delusion that sometime they could manage to get two rations of bread out of the tray. But in my experience that sometime never came. The club of the First Hall-man had a way of flashing out—quick as the stroke of a tiger's claw—to the hand that dared ambitiously. The First Hall-man was a good judge of distance, and he had smashed so many hands with that club that he had become infallible. He never missed, and he usually punished the offending convict by taking his one ration away from him and sending him to his cell to make his meal off of hot water.

And at times, while all these men lay hungry in their cells, I have seen a hundred or so extra rations of bread hidden away in the cells of the hall-men. It would seem absurd, our retaining this bread. But it was one of our grafts. We were economic masters inside our hall, turning the trick in ways quite similar to the economic masters of civilization. We controlled the food-supply of the population, and, just like our brother bandits outside, we made the people pay through the nose for it. We peddled the bread. Once a week, the men who worked in the yard received a five-cent plug of chewing tobacco. This chewing tobacco was the coin of the realm. Two or three rations of bread for a plug was the way we exchanged, and they traded, not because they loved tobacco less, but because they loved bread more. Oh, I know, it was like taking candy from a baby, but what would you? We had to live. And certainly there should be some reward for initiative and enterprise. Besides, we but patterned ourselves after our betters outside the walls, who, on a larger scale, and under the respectable disguise of merchants, bankers, and captains of industry, did precisely what we were doing. What awful things would have happened to those poor wretches if it hadn't been for us, I can't imagine. Heaven knows we put bread into circulation in the Erie County Pen. Ay, and we encouraged frugality and thrift… in the poor devils who forewent their tobacco. And then there was our example. In the breast of every convict there we implanted the ambition to become even as we and run a graft. Saviours of society—I guess yes.

Here was a hungry man without any tobacco. Maybe he was a profligate and had used it all up on himself. Very good; he had a pair of suspenders. I exchanged half a dozen rations of bread for it—or a dozen rations if the suspenders were very good. Now I never wore suspenders, but that didn't matter. Around the corner lodged a long-timer, doing ten years for manslaughter. He wore suspenders, and he wanted a pair. I could trade them to him for some of his meat. Meat was what I wanted. Or perhaps he had a tattered, paper-covered novel. That was treasure-trove. I could read it and then trade it off to the bakers for cake, or to the cooks for meat and vegetables, or to the firemen for decent coffee, or to some one or other for the newspaper that occasionally filtered in, heaven alone knows how. The cooks, bakers, and firemen were prisoners like myself, and they lodged in our hall in the first row of cells over us.

In short, a full-grown system of barter obtained in the Erie County Pen. There was even money in circulation. This money was sometimes smuggled in by the short-timers, more frequently came from the barber-shop graft, where the newcomers were mulcted, but most of all flowed from the cells of the long-timers—though how they got it I don't know.

What of his pre-eminent position, the First Hall-man was reputed to be quite wealthy. In addition to his miscellaneous grafts, he grafted on us. We farmed the general wretchedness, and the First Hall-man was Farmer-General over all of us. We held our particular grafts by his permission, and we had to pay for that permission. As I say, he was reputed to be wealthy; but we never saw his money, and he lived in a cell all to himself in solitary grandeur.

But that money was made in the Pen I had direct evidence, for I was cell-mate quite a time with the Third Hall-man. He had over sixteen dollars. He used to count his money every night after nine o'clock, when we were locked in. Also, he used to tell me each night what he would do to me if I gave away on him to the other hall-men. You see, he was afraid of being robbed, and danger threatened him from three different directions. There were the guards. A couple of them might jump upon him, give him a good beating for alleged insubordination, and throw him into the 'solitaire' (the dungeon); and in the mix-up that sixteen dollars of his would take wings. Then again, the First Hall-man could have taken it all away from him by threatening to dismiss him and fire him back to hard labour in the prison-yard. And yet again, there were the ten of us who were ordinary hall-men. If we got an inkling of his wealth, there was a large liability, some quiet day, of the whole bunch of us getting him into a corner and dragging him down. Oh, we were wolves, believe me—just like the fellows who do business in Wall Street.

He had good reason to be afraid of us, and so had I to be afraid of him. He was a huge, illiterate brute, an ex-Chesapeake-Bay-oyster-pirate, an 'ex-con' who had done five years in Sing Sing, and a general all-around stupidly carnivorous beast. He used to trap sparrows that flew into our hall through the open bars. When he made a capture, he hurried away with it into his cell, where I have seen him crunching bones and spitting out feathers as he bolted it raw. Oh, no, I never gave away on him to the other hall-men. This is the first time I have mentioned his sixteen dollars.

But I grafted on him just the same. He was in love with a woman prisoner who was confined in the 'female department'. He could neither read nor write, and I used to read her letters to him and write his replies. And I made him pay for it, too. But they were good letters. I laid myself out on them, put in my best licks, and furthermore, I won her for him; though I shrewdly guess that she was in love, not with him, but with the humble scribe. I repeat, those letters were great.

Another one of our grafts was 'passing the punk'. We were the celestial messengers, the fire-bringers, in that iron world of bolt and bar. When the men came in from work at night and were locked in their cells, they wanted to smoke. Then it was that we restored the divine spark, running the galleries, from cell to cell, with our smouldering punks. Those who were wise, or with whom we did business, had their punks all ready to light. Not every one got divine sparks, however. The guy who refused to dig up, went sparkless and smokeless to bed. But what did we care? We had the immortal cinch on him, and if he got fresh, two or three of us would pitch on him and give him 'what-for'.

You see, this was the working theory of the hall-men. There were thirteen of us. We had something like half a thousand prisoners in our hall. We were supposed to do the work, and to keep order. The latter was the function of the guards, which they turned over to us. It was up to us to keep order; if we didn't, we'd be fired back to hard labour, most probably with a taste of the dungeon thrown in. But so long as we maintained order, that long could we work our own particular grafts.

Bear with me a moment and look at the problem. Here were thirteen beasts of us over half a thousand other beasts. It was a living hell, that prison, and it was up to us thirteen there to rule. It was impossible, considering the nature of the beasts, for us to rule by kindness. We ruled by fear. Of course, behind us, backing us up, were the guards. In extremity we called upon them for help; but it would bother them if we called upon them too often, in which event we could depend upon it that they would get more efficient trusties to take our places. But we did not call upon them often, except in a quiet sort of way, when we wanted a cell unlocked in order to get at a refractory prisoner inside. In such cases all the guard did was to unlock the door and walk away so as not to be a witness of what happened when half a dozen hall-men went inside and did a bit of manhandling.

As regards the details of this manhandling I shall say nothing. And after all, manhandling was merely one of the very minor unprintable horrors of the Erie County Pen. I say 'unprintable'; and in justice I must also say 'unthinkable'. They were unthinkable to me until I saw them, and I was no spring chicken in the ways of the world and the awful abysses of human degradation. It would take a deep plummet to reach bottom in the Erie County Pen, and I do but skim lightly and facetiously the surface of things as I there saw them.

At times, say in the morning when the prisoners came down to wash, the thirteen of us would be practically alone in the midst of them, and every last one of them had it in for us. Thirteen against five hundred, and we ruled by fear. We could not permit the slightest infraction of rules, the slightest insolence. If we did, we were lost. Our own rule was to hit a man as soon as he opened his mouth—hit him hard, hit him with anything. A broom-handle, end-on, in the face, had a very sobering effect. But that was not all. Such a man must be made an example of; so the next rule was to wade right in and follow him up. Of course, one was sure that every hall-man in sight would come on the run to join in the chastisement; for this also was a rule. Whenever any hall-man was in trouble with a prisoner, the duty of any other hall-man who happened to be around was to lend a fist. Never mind the merits of the case—wade in and hit, and hit with anything; in short, lay the man out.

I remember a handsome young mulatto of about twenty who got the insane idea into his head that he should stand for his rights. And he did have the right of it, too; but that didn't help him any. He lived on the topmost gallery. Eight hall-men took the conceit out of him in just about a minute and a half—for that was the length of time required to travel along his gallery to the end and down five flights of steel stairs. He travelled the whole distance on every portion of his anatomy except his feet, and the eight hall-men were not idle. The mulatto struck the pavement where I was standing watching it all. He regained his feet and stood upright for a moment. In that moment he threw his arms wide apart and omitted an awful scream of terror and pain and heartbreak. At the same instant, as in a transformation scene, the shreds of his stout prison clothes fell from him, leaving him wholly naked and streaming blood from every portion of the surface of his body. Then he collapsed in a heap, unconscious. He had learned his lesson, and every convict within those walls who heard him scream had learned a lesson. So had I learned mine. it is not a nice thing to see a man's heart broken in a minute and a half.

The following will illustrate how we drummed up business in the graft of passing the punk. A row of newcomers is installed in your cells. You pass along before the bars with your punk. 'Hey, Bo, give us a light,' someone calls to you. Now this is an advertisement that that particular man has tobacco on him. You pass in the punk and go your way. A little later you come back and lean up casually against the bars. 'Say, Bo, can you let us have a little tobacco?' is what you say. If he is not wise to the game, the chances are that he solemnly avers that he hasn't any more tobacco. All very well. You condole with him and go your way. But you know that his punk will last him only the rest of that day. Next day you come by, and he says again, 'Hey, Bo, give us a light.' And you say, 'You haven't any tobacco and you don't need a light.' And you don't give him any, either. Half an hour after, or an hour or two or three hours, you will be passing by and the man will call out to you in mild tones, 'Come here, Bo.' And you come. You thrust your hand between the bars and have it filled with precious tobacco. Then you give him a light.

Sometimes, however, a newcomer arrives, upon whom no grafts are to be worked. The mysterious word is passed along that he is to be treated decently. Where this word originated I could never learn. The one thing patent is that the man has a 'pull'. It may be with one of the superior hall-men; it may be with one of the guards in some other part of the prison; it may be that good treatment has been purchased from grafters higher up; but be it as it may, we know that it is up to us to treat him decently if we want to avoid trouble.

We hall-men were middlemen and common carriers. We arranged trades between convicts confined in different parts of the prison, and we put through the exchange. Also, we took our commissions coming and going. Sometimes the objects traded had to go through the hands of half a dozen middlemen, each of whom took his whack, or in some way or another was paid for his service.

Sometimes one was in debt for services, and sometimes one had others in his debt. Thus, I entered the prison in debt to the convict who smuggled in my things for me. A week or so afterward, one of the firemen passed a letter into my hand. It had been given to him by a barber. The barber had received it from the convict who had smuggled in my things. Because of my debt to him I was to carry the letter on. But he had not written the letter. The original sender was a long-timer in his hall. The letter was for a woman prisoner in the female department. But whether it was intended for her, or whether she, in turn, was one of the chain of go-betweens, I did not know. All that I knew was her description, and that it was up to me to get it into her hands.

Two days passed, during which time I kept the letter in my possession; then the opportunity came. The women did the mending of all the clothes worn by the convicts. A number of our hall-men had to go to the female department to bring back huge bundles of clothes. I fixed it with the First Hall-man that I was to go along. Door after door was unlocked for us as we threaded our way across the prison to the women's quarters. We entered a large room where the women sat working at their mending. My eyes were peeled for the woman who had been described to me. I located her and worked near to her. Two eagle-eyed matrons were on watch. I held the letter in my palm, and I looked my intention at the woman. She knew I had something for her; she must have been expecting it, and had set herself to divining, at the moment we entered, which of us was the messenger. But one of the matrons stood within two feet of her. Already the hall-men were picking up the bundles they were to carry away. The moment was passing. I delayed with my bundle, making believe that it was not tied securely. Would that matron ever look away? Or was I to fail? And just then another woman cut up playfully with one of the hall-men—stuck out her foot and tripped him, or pinched him, or did something or other. The matron looked that way and reprimanded the woman sharply. Now I do not know whether or not this was all planned to distract the matron's attention, but I did know that it was my opportunity. My particular woman's hand dropped from her lap down by her side. I stooped to pick up my bundle. From my stooping position I slipped the letter into her hand, and received another in exchange. The next moment the bundle was on my shoulder, the matron's gaze had returned to me because I was the last hall-man, and I was hastening to catch up with my companions. The letter I had received from the woman I turned over to the fireman, and thence it passed through the hands of the barber, of the convict who had smuggled in my things, and on to the long-timer at the other end.

Often we conveyed letters, the chain of communication of which was so complex that we knew neither sender nor sendee. We were but links in the chain. Somewhere, somehow, a convict would thrust a letter into my hand with the instruction to pass it on to the next link. All such acts were favours to be reciprocated later on, when I should be acting directly with a principal in transmitting letters, and from whom I should be receiving my pay. The whole prison was covered by a network of lines of communication. And we who were in control of the system of communication, naturally, since we were modelled after capitalistic society, exacted heavy tolls from our customers. It was service for profit with a vengeance, though we were at times not above giving service for love.

And all the time I was in the Pen I was making myself solid with my pal. He had done much for me, and in return he expected me to do as much for him. When we got out, we were to travel together, and, it goes without saying, pull off 'jobs' together. For my pal was a criminal—oh, not a jewel of the first water, merely a petty criminal who would steal and rob, commit burglary, and, if cornered, not stop short of murder. Many a quiet hour we sat and talked together. He had two or three jobs in view for the immediate future, in which my work was cut out for me, and in which I joined in planning the details. I had been with and seen much of criminals, and my pal never dreamed that I was only fooling him, giving him a string thirty days long. He thought I was the real goods, liked me because I was not stupid, and liked me a bit, too, I think, for myself. Of course I had not the slightest intention of joining him in a life of sordid, petty crime; but I'd have been an idiot to throw away all the good things his friendship made possible. When one is on the hot lava of hell, he cannot pick and choose his path, and so it was with me in the Erie County Pen. I had to stay in with the 'push', or do hard labour on bread and water; and to stay in with the push I had to make good with my pal.

Life was not monotonous in the Pen. Every day something was happening: men were having fits, going crazy, fighting, or the hall-men were getting drunk. Rover Jack, one of the ordinary hall-men, was our star 'oryide'. He was a true 'profesh', a 'blowed-in-the-glass' stiff, and as such received all kinds of latitude from the hall-men in authority. Pittsburg Joe, who was Second Hall-man, used to join Rover Jack in his jags; and it was a saying of the pair that the Erie County Pen was the only place where a man could get 'slopped' and not be arrested. I never knew, but I was told that bromide of potassium, gained in devious ways from the dispensary, was the dope they used. But I do know, whatever their dope was, that they got good and drunk on occasion.

Our hall was a common stews, filled with the ruck and the filth, the scum and dregs, of society—hereditary inefficients, degenerates, wrecks, lunatics, addled intelligences, epileptics, monsters, weaklings, in short, a very nightmare of humanity. Hence, fits flourished with us. These fits seemed contagious.

When one man began throwing a fit, others followed his lead. I have seen seven men down with fits at the same time, making the air hideous with their cries, while as many more lunatics would be raging and gibbering up and down. Nothing was ever done for the men with fits except to throw cold water on them. It was useless to send for the medical student or the doctor. They were not to be bothered with such trivial and frequent occurrences.

There was a young Dutch boy, about eighteen years of age, who had fits most frequently of all. He usually threw one every day. It was for that reason that we kept him on the ground floor farther down in the row of cells in which we lodged. After he had had a few fits in the prison-yard, the guards refused to be bothered with him any more, and so he remained locked up in his cell all day with a Cockney cell-mate, to keep him company. Not that the Cockney was of any use. Whenever the Dutch boy had a fit, the Cockney became paralyzed with terror.

The Dutch boy could not speak a word of English. He was a farmer's boy, serving ninety days as punishment for having got into a scrap with someone. He prefaced his fits with howling. He howled like a wolf. Also, he took his fits standing up, which was very inconvenient for him, for his fits always culminated in a headlong pitch to the floor. Whenever I heard the long wolf-howl rising, I used to grab a broom and run to his cell. Now the trusties were not allowed keys to the cells, so I could not get in to him. He would stand up in the middle of his narrow cell, shivering convulsively, his eyes rolled backward till only the whites were visible, and howling like a lost soul. Try as I would, I could never get the Cockney to lend him a hand. While he stood and howled, the Cockney crouched and trembled in the upper bunk, his terror-stricken gaze fixed on that awful figure, with eyes rolled back, that howled and howled. It was hard on him, too, the poor devil of a Cockney. His own reason was not any too firmly seated, and the wonder is that he did not go mad.

All that I could do was my best with the broom. I would thrust it through the bars, train it on Dutchy's chest, and wait. As the crisis approached he would begin swaying back and forth. I followed this swaying with the broom, for there was no telling when he would take that dreadful forward pitch. But when he did, I was there with the broom, catching him and easing him down. Contrive as I would, he never came down quite gently, and his face was usually bruised by the stone floor. Once down and writhing in convulsions, I'd throw a bucket of water over him. I don't know whether cold water was the right thing or not, but it was the custom in the Erie County Pen. Nothing more than that was ever done for him. He would lie there, wet, for an hour or so, and then crawl into his bunk. I knew better than to run to a guard for assistance. What was a man with a fit, anyway?

In the adjoining cell lived a strange character—a man who was doing sixty days for eating swill out of Barnum's swill-barrel, or at least that was the way he put it. He was a badly addled creature, and, at first, very mild and gentle. The facts of his case were as he had stated them. He had strayed out to the circus ground, and, being hungry, had made his way to the barrel that contained the refuse from the table of the circus people. 'And it was good bread,' he often assured me; 'and the meat was out of sight.' A policeman had seen him and arrested him, and there he was.

Once I passed his cell with a piece of stiff thin wire in my hand. He asked me for it so earnestly that I passed it through the bars to him. Promptly, and with no tool but his fingers, he broke it into short lengths and twisted them into half a dozen very creditable safety pins. He sharpened the points on the stone floor. Thereafter I did quite a trade in safety pins. I furnished the raw material and peddled the finished product, and he did the work. As wages, I paid him extra rations of bread, and once in a while a chunk of meat or a piece of soup-bone with some marrow inside.

But his imprisonment told on him, and he grew violent day

by day. The hall-men took delight in teasing him. They filled his weak brain with stories of a great fortune that had been left him. It was in order to rob him of it that he had been arrested and sent to jail. Of course, as he himself knew, there was no law against eating out of a barrel. Therefore he was wrongly imprisoned. It was a plot to deprive him of his fortune.

The first I knew of it, I heard the hall-men laughing about the string they had given him. Next he held a serious conference with me, in which he told me of his millions and the plot to deprive him of them, and in which he appointed me his detective. I did my best to let him down gently, speaking vaguely of a mistake, and that it was another man with a similar name who was the rightful heir. I left him quite cooled down; but I couldn't keep the hall-men away from him, and they continued to string him worse than ever. In the end, after a most violent scene, he threw me down, revoked my private detectiveship, and went on strike. My trade in safety pins ceased. He refused to make any more safety pins, and he peppered me with raw material through the bars of his cell when I passed by.

I could never make it up with him. The other hall-men told him that I was a detective in the employ of the conspirators. And in the meantime the hall-men drove him mad with their stringing. His fictitious wrongs preyed upon his mind, and at last he became a dangerous and homicidal lunatic. The guards refused to listen to his tale of stolen millions, and he accused them of being in the plot. One day he threw a pannikin of hot tea over one of them, and then his case was investigated. The warden talked with him a few minutes through the bars of his cell. Then he was taken away for examination before the doctors. He never came back, and I often wonder if he is dead, or if he still gibbers about his millions in some asylum for the insane.

At last came the day of days, my release. It was the day of release for the Third Hall-man as well, and the short-timer girl I had won for him was waiting for him outside the wall. They went away blissfully together. My pal and I went out together, and together we walked down into Buffalo. Were we not to be together always? We begged together on the 'main-drag' that day for pennies, and what we received was spent for 'shupers' of beer—I don't know how they are spelled, but they are pronounced the way I have spelled them, and they cost three cents. I was watching my chance all the time for a get-away. From some bo on the drag I managed to learn what time a certain freight pulled out. I calculated my time accordingly. When the moment came, my pal and I were in a saloon. Two foaming shupers were before us. I'd have liked to say goodbye. He had been good to me. But I did not dare. I went out through the rear of the saloon and jumped the fence. It was a swift sneak, and a few minutes later I was on board a freight and heading south on the Western New York and Pennsylvania Railroad.

10

THE SON OF THE WOLF

Man rarely places a proper valuation upon his womankind, at least not until deprived of them. He has no conception of the subtle atmosphere exhaled by the sex feminine, so long as he bathes in it; but let it be withdrawn, and an ever-growing void begins to manifest itself in his existence, and he becomes hungry, in a vague sort of way, for a something so indefinite that he cannot characterize it. If his comrades have no more experience than himself, they will shake their heads dubiously and dose him with strong physic. But the hunger will continue and become stronger; he will lose interest in the things of his everyday life and wax morbid; and one day, when the emptiness has become unbearable, a revelation will dawn upon him.

In the Yukon country, when this comes to pass, the man usually provisions a poling boat, if it is summer, and if winter, harnesses his dogs, and heads for the Southland. A few months later, supposing him to be possessed of a faith in the country, he returns with a wife to share with him in that faith, and incidentally in his hardships. This but serves to show the innate selfishness of man. It also brings us to the trouble of 'Scruff' Mackenzie, which occurred in the old days, before the country was stampeded and staked by a tidal wave of the che-cha-quas, and when the Klondike's only claim to notice was its salmon fisheries.

'Scruff' Mackenzie bore the earmarks of a frontier birth and a frontier life. His face was stamped with twenty-five years of incessant struggle with Nature in her wildest moods,—the last two, the wildest and hardest of all, having been spent in groping for the gold which lies in the shadow of the Arctic Circle. When the yearning sickness came upon him, he was not surprised, for he was a practical man and had seen other men thus stricken. But he showed no sign of his malady, save that he worked harder. All summer he fought mosquitoes and washed the sure-thing bars of the Stuart River for a double grubstake. Then he floated a raft of houselogs down the Yukon to Forty Mile, and put together as comfortable a cabin as any the camp could boast of. In fact, it showed such cosy promise that many men elected to be his partner and to come and live with him. But he crushed their aspirations with rough speech, peculiar for its strength and brevity, and bought a double supply of grub from the trading-post.

As has been noted, 'Scruff' Mackenzie was a practical man. If he wanted a thing he usually got it, but in doing so, went no farther out of his way than was necessary. Though a son of toil and hardship, he was averse to a journey of six hundred miles on the ice, a second of two thousand miles on the ocean, and still a third thousand miles or so to his last stamping-grounds—all in the mere quest of a wife. Life was too short. So he rounded up his dogs, lashed a curious freight to his sled, and faced across the divide whose westward slopes were drained by the head-reaches of the Tanana.

He was a sturdy traveller, and his wolf-dogs could work harder and travel farther on less grub than any other team in the Yukon. Three weeks later he strode into a hunting-camp of the Upper Tanana Sticks. They marvelled at his temerity; for they had a bad name and had been known to kill white men for as trifling a thing as a sharp axe or a broken rifle. But he went among them single-handed, his bearing being a delicious composite of humility, familiarity, sang-froid, and insolence. It required a deft hand and deep knowledge of the barbaric mind effectually to handle such diverse weapons; but he was a past-master in the art, knowing when to conciliate and when to threaten with Jove-like wrath.

He first made obeisance to the Chief Thling-Tinneh, presenting him with a couple of pounds of black tea and tobacco, and thereby winning his most cordial regard. Then he mingled with the men and maidens, and that night gave a potlach. The snow was beaten down in the form of an oblong, perhaps a hundred feet in length and quarter as many across. Down the centre a log fire was built, while either side was carpeted with spruce boughs. The lodges were forsaken, and the fivescore or so members of the tribe gave tongue to their folk-chants in honour of their guest.

'Scruff' Mackenzie's two years had taught him the not many hundred words of their vocabulary, and he had likewise conquered their deep gutturals, their Japanese idioms, constructions, and honorific and agglutinative particles. So he made oration after their manner, satisfying their instinctive poetry-love with crude flights of eloquence and metaphorical contortions. After Thling-Tinneh and the Shaman had responded in kind, he made trifling presents to the menfolk, joined in their singing, and proved an expert in their fifty-two-stick gambling game.

And they smoked his tobacco and were pleased. But among the younger men there was a defiant attitude, a spirit of braggadocio, easily understood by the raw insinuations of the toothless squaws and the giggling of the maidens. They had known few white men, 'Sons of the Wolf', but from those few they had learned strange lessons.

Nor had 'Scruff' Mackenzie, for all his seeming carelessness, failed to note these phenomena. In truth, rolled in his sleeping-furs, he thought it all over, thought seriously, and emptied many pipes in mapping out a campaign. One maiden only had caught his fancy—none other than Zarinska, daughter to the chief. In features, form, and poise, answering more nearly to the white man's type of beauty, she was almost an anomaly among her tribal sisters. He would possess her, make her his wife, and name her—ah, he would name her Gertrude! Having thus decided, he rolled over on his side and dropped off to sleep, a true son of his all-conquering race, a Samson among the Philistines.

It was slow work and a stiff game; but 'Scruff' Mackenzie manoeuvred cunningly, with an unconcern which served to puzzle the Sticks. He took great care to impress the men that he was a sure shot and a mighty hunter, and the camp rang with his plaudits when he brought down a moose at six hundred yards. Of a night he visited in Chief Thling-Tinneh's lodge of moose and caribou skins, talking big and dispensing tobacco with a lavish hand. Nor did he fail to likewise honour the Shaman; for he realized the medicine-man's influence with his people, and was anxious to make of him an ally. But that worthy was high and mighty, refused to be propitiated, and was unerringly marked down as a prospective enemy.

Though no opening presented for an interview with Zarinska, Mackenzie stole many a glance to her, giving fair warning of his intent. And well she knew, yet coquettishly surrounded herself with a ring of women whenever the men were away and he had a chance. But he was in no hurry; besides, he knew she could not help but think of him, and a few days of such thought would only better his suit.

At last, one night, when he deemed the time to be ripe, he abruptly left the chief's smoky dwelling and hastened to a neighbouring lodge. As usual, she sat with squaws and maidens about her, all engaged in sewing moccasins and beadwork. They laughed at his entrance, and badinage, which linked Zarinska to him, ran high. But one after the other they were unceremoniously bundled into the outer snow, whence they hurried to spread the tale through all the camp.

His cause was well pleaded, in her tongue, for she did not know his, and at the end of two hours he rose to go.

'So Zarinska will come to the White Man's lodge? Good! I go now to have talk with thy father, for he may not be so minded. And I will give him many tokens; but he must not ask too much. If he say no? Good! Zarinska shall yet come to the White Man's lodge.'

He had already lifted the skin flap to depart, when a low exclamation brought him back to the girl's side. She brought herself to her knees on the bearskin mat, her face aglow with true Eve-light, and shyly unbuckled his heavy belt. He looked down, perplexed, suspicious, his ears alert for the slightest sound without. But her next move disarmed his doubt, and he smiled with pleasure. She took from her sewing bag a moosehide sheath, brave with bright beadwork, fantastically designed. She drew his great hunting-knife, gazed reverently along the keen edge, half tempted to try it with her thumb, and shot it into place in its new home. Then she slipped the sheath along the belt to its customary resting-place, just above the hip.

For all the world, it was like a scene of olden time—a lady and her knight. Mackenzie drew her up full height and swept her red lips with his moustache—the, to her, foreign caress of the Wolf. It was a meeting of the stone age and the steel; but she was none the less a woman, as her crimson cheeks and the luminous softness of her eyes attested.

There was a thrill of excitement in the air as 'Scruff' Mackenzie, a bulky bundle under his arm, threw open the flap of Thling-Tinneh's tent. Children were running about in the open, dragging dry wood to the scene of the potlach, a babble of women's voices was growing in intensity, the young men were consulting in sullen groups, while from the Shaman's lodge rose the eerie sounds of an incantation.

The chief was alone with his blear-eyed wife, but a glance

sufficed to tell Mackenzie that the news was already told. So he plunged at once into the business, shifting the beaded sheath prominently to the fore as advertisement of the betrothal.

'O Thling-Tinneh, mighty chief of the Sticks and the land of the Tanana, ruler of the salmon and the bear, the moose and the caribou! The White Man is before thee with a great purpose. Many moons has his lodge been empty, and he is lonely. And his heart has eaten itself in silence, and grown hungry for a woman to sit beside him in his lodge, to meet him from the hunt with warm fire and good food. He has heard strange things, the patter of baby moccasins and the sound of children's voices. And one night a vision came upon him, and he beheld the Raven, who is thy father, the great Raven, who is the father of all the Sticks. And the Raven spake to the lonely White Man, saying: "Bind thou thy moccasins upon thee, and gird thy snowshoes on, and lash thy sled with food for many sleeps and fine tokens for the Chief Thling-Tinneh. For thou shalt turn thy face to where the midspring sun is wont to sink below the land and journey to this great chief's hunting-grounds. There thou shalt make big presents, and Thling-Tinneh, who is my son, shall become to thee as a father. In his lodge there is a maiden into whom I breathed the breath of life for thee. This maiden shalt thou take to wife."

'O Chief, thus spake the great Raven; thus do I lay many presents at thy feet; thus am I come to take thy daughter!'

The old man drew his furs about him with crude consciousness of royalty, but delayed reply while a youngster crept in, delivered a quick message to appear before the council, and was gone.

'O White Man, whom we have named Moose-Killer, also known as the Wolf, and the Son of the Wolf! We know thou comest of a mighty race; we are proud to have thee our potlach-guest; but the king-salmon does not mate with the dog-salmon, nor the Raven with the Wolf.'

'Not so!' cried Mackenzie. 'The daughters of the Raven have I met in the camps of the Wolf—the squaw of Mortimer, the squaw of Tregidgo, the squaw of Barnaby, who came two ice-runs back, and I have heard of other squaws, though my eyes beheld them not.'

'Son, your words are true; but it were evil mating, like the water with the sand, like the snowflake with the sun. But met you one Mason and his squaw' No? He came ten ice-runs ago.—The first of all the Wolves. And with him there was a mighty man, straight as a willow-shoot, and tall; strong as the bald-faced grizzly, with a heart like the full summer moon; his—'

'Oh!' interrupted Mackenzie, recognizing the well-known Northland figure, 'Malemute Kid!'

'The same—a mighty man. But saw you aught of the squaw? She was full sister to Zarinska.'

'Nay, Chief; but I have heard. Mason—far, far to the north, a spruce-tree, heavy with years, crushed out his life beneath. But his love was great, and he had much gold. With this, and her boy, she journeyed countless sleeps toward the winter's noonday sun, and there she yet lives—no biting frost, no snow, no summer's midnight sun, no winter's noonday night.'

A second messenger interrupted with imperative summons from the council. As Mackenzie threw him into the snow, he caught a glimpse of the swaying forms before the council-fire, heard the deep basses of the men in rhythmic chant, and knew the Shaman was fanning the anger of his people. Time pressed. He turned upon the chief.

'Come! I wish thy child. And now, see! Here are tobacco, tea, many cups of sugar, warm blankets, handkerchiefs, both good and large; and here, a true rifle, with many bullets and much powder.'

'Nay,' replied the old man, struggling against the great wealth spread before him. 'Even now are my people come together. They will not have this marriage.'

'But thou art chief.'

'Yet do my young men rage because the Wolves have taken their maidens so that they may not marry.'

'Listen, O Thling-Tinneh! Ere the night has passed into the day, the Wolf shall face his dogs to the Mountains of the East and fare forth to the Country of the Yukon. And Zarinska shall break trail for his dogs.'

'And ere the night has gained its middle, my young men may fling to the dogs the flesh of the Wolf, and his bones be scattered in the snow till the springtime lay them bare.'

It was threat and counter-threat. Mackenzie's bronzed face flushed darkly. He raised his voice. The old squaw, who till now had sat an impassive spectator, made to creep by him for the door. The song of the men broke suddenly and there was a hubbub of many voices as he whirled the old woman roughly to her couch of skins.

'Again I cry—listen, O Thling-Tinneh! The Wolf dies with teeth fast-locked, and with him there shall sleep ten of thy strongest men—men who are needed, for the hunting is not begun, and the fishing is not many moons away. And again, of what profit should I die? I know the custom of thy people; thy share of my wealth shall be very small. Grant me thy child, and it shall all be thine. And yet again, my brothers will come, and they are many, and their maws are never filled; and the daughters of the Raven shall bear children in the lodges of the Wolf. My people are greater than thy people. It is destiny. Grant, and all this wealth is thine.'

Moccasins were crunching the snow without. Mackenzie threw his rifle to cock, and loosened the twin Colts in his belt.

'Grant, O Chief!'

'And yet will my people say no.'

'Grant, and the wealth is thine. Then shall I deal with thy people after.'

'The Wolf will have it so. I will take his tokens—but I would warn him.'

Mackenzie passed over the goods, taking care to clog the rifle's ejector, and capping the bargain with a kaleidoscopic silk kerchief. The Shaman and half a dozen young braves entered, but he shouldered boldly among them and passed out.

'Pack!' was his laconic greeting to Zarinska as he passed her lodge and hurried to harness his dogs. A few minutes later he swept into the council at the head of the team, the woman by his side. He took his place at the upper end of the oblong, by the side of the chief. To his left, a step to the rear, he stationed Zarinska—her proper place. Besides, the time was ripe for mischief, and there was need to guard his back.

On either side, the men crouched to the fire, their voices lifted in a folk-chant out of the forgotten past. Full of strange, halting cadences and haunting recurrences, it was not beautiful. 'Fearful' may inadequately express it. At the lower end, under the eye of the Shaman, danced half a score of women. Stern were his reproofs of those who did not wholly abandon themselves to the ecstasy of the rite. Half hidden in their heavy masses of raven hair, all dishevelled and falling to their waists, they slowly swayed to and fro, their forms rippling to an ever-changing rhythm.

It was a weird scene; an anachronism. To the south, the nineteenth century was reeling off the few years of its last decade; here flourished man primeval, a shade removed from the prehistoric cave-dweller, forgotten fragment of the Elder World. The tawny wolf-dogs sat between their skin-clad masters or fought for room, the firelight cast backward from their red eyes and dripping fangs. The woods, in ghostly shroud, slept on unheeding. The White Silence, for the moment driven to the rimming forest, seemed ever crushing inward; the stars danced with great leaps, as is their wont in the time of the Great Cold; while the Spirits of the Pole trailed their robes of glory athwart the heavens.

'Scruff' Mackenzie dimly realized the wild grandeur of the setting as his eyes ranged down the fur-fringed sides in quest of missing faces. They rested for a moment on a newborn babe, suckling at its mother's naked breast. It was forty below—seven and odd degrees of frost. He thought of the tender women of his own race and smiled grimly. Yet from the loins of some such tender woman had he sprung with a kingly inheritance—an inheritance which gave to him and his dominance over the land and sea, over the animals and the peoples of all the zones. Single-handed against fivescore, girt by the Arctic winter, far from his own, he felt the prompting of his heritage, the desire to possess, the wild danger-love, the thrill of battle, the power to conquer or to die.

The singing and the dancing ceased, and the Shaman flared up in rude eloquence. Through the sinuosities of their vast mythology, he worked cunningly upon the credulity of his people. The case was strong. Opposing the creative principles as embodied in the Crow and the Raven, he stigmatized Mackenzie as the Wolf, the fighting and the destructive principle. Not only was the combat of these forces spiritual, but men fought, each to his totem. They were the children of Jelchs, the Raven, the Promethean fire-bringer; Mackenzie was the child of the Wolf, or in other words, the Devil. For them to bring a truce to this perpetual warfare, to marry their daughters to the arch-enemy, were treason and blasphemy of the highest order. No phrase was harsh nor figure vile enough in branding Mackenzie as a sneaking interloper and emissary of Satan. There was a subdued, savage roar in the deep chests of his listeners as he took the swing of his peroration.

'Aye, my brothers, Jelchs is all-powerful! Did he not bring heaven-borne fire that we might be warm? Did he not draw the sun, moon, and stars, from their holes that we might see? Did he not teach us that we might fight the Spirits of Famine and of Frost? But now Jelchs is angry with his children, and they are grown to a handful, and he will not help. For they have forgotten him, and done evil things, and trod bad trails, and taken his enemies into their lodges to sit by their fires. And the Raven is sorrowful at the wickedness of his children; but when they shall rise up and show they have come back, he will come out of the darkness to aid them. O brothers! the Fire-Bringer has whispered messages to thy Shaman; the same shall ye hear. Let the young men take the young women to their lodges; let them fly at the throat of the Wolf; let them be undying in their enmity! Then shall their women become fruitful and they shall multiply into a mighty people! And the Raven shall lead great tribes of their fathers and their fathers' fathers from out of the North; and they shall beat back the Wolves till they are as last year's campfires; and they shall again come to rule over all the land! 'Tis the message of Jelchs, the Raven.'

This foreshadowing of the Messiah's coming brought a hoarse howl from the Sticks as they leaped to their feet. Mackenzie slipped the thumbs of his mittens and waited. There was a clamour for the 'Fox', not to be stilled till one of the young men stepped forward to speak.

'Brothers! The Shaman has spoken wisely. The Wolves have taken our women, and our men are childless. We are grown to a handful. The Wolves have taken our warm furs and given for them evil spirits which dwell in bottles, and clothes which come not from the beaver or the lynx, but are made from the grass. And they are not warm, and our men die of strange sicknesses. I, the Fox, have taken no woman to wife; and why? Twice have the maidens which pleased me gone to the camps of the Wolf. Even now have I laid by skins of the beaver, of the moose, of the caribou, that I might win favour in the eyes of Thling-Tinneh, that I might marry Zarinska, his daughter. Even now are her snowshoes bound to her feet, ready to break trail for the dogs of the Wolf. Nor do I speak for myself alone. As I have done, so has the Bear. He, too, had fain been the father of her children, and many skins has he cured thereto. I speak for all the young men who know not wives. The Wolves are ever hungry. Always do they take the choice meat at the killing. To the Ravens are left the leavings.

'There is Gugkla,' he cried, brutally pointing out one of the women, who was a cripple. 'Her legs are bent like the ribs of a birch canoe. She cannot gather wood nor carry the meat of the hunters. Did the Wolves choose her?'

'Ai! ai!' vociferated his tribesmen.

'There is Moyri, whose eyes are crossed by the Evil Spirit. Even the babes are affrighted when they gaze upon her, and it is said the bald-face gives her the trail. Was she chosen?'

Again the cruel applause rang out.

'And there sits Pischet. She does not hearken to my words. Never has she heard the cry of the chit-chat, the voice of her husband, the babble of her child. She lives in the White Silence. Cared the Wolves aught for her? No! Theirs is the choice of the kill; ours is the leavings.

'Brothers, it shall not be! No more shall the Wolves slink among our campfires. The time is come.'

A great streamer of fire, the aurora borealis, purple, green, and yellow, shot across the zenith, bridging horizon to horizon. With head thrown back and arms extended, he swayed to his climax.

'Behold! The spirits of our fathers have arisen and great deeds are afoot this night!'

He stepped back, and another young man somewhat diffidently came forward, pushed on by his comrades. He towered a full head above them, his broad chest defiantly bared to the frost. He swung tentatively from one foot to the other. Words halted upon his tongue, and he was ill at ease. His face was horrible to look upon, for it had at one time been half torn away by some terrific blow. At last he struck his breast with his clenched fist, drawing sound as from a drum, and his voice rumbled forth as does the surf from an ocean cavern.

'I am the Bear—the Silver-Tip and the Son of the Silver-Tip! When my voice was yet as a girl's, I slew the lynx, the moose, and the caribou; when it whistled like the wolverines from under a cache, I crossed the Mountains of the South and slew three of the White Rivers; when it became as the roar of the Chinook, I met the bald-faced grizzly, but gave no trail.'

At this he paused, his hand significantly sweeping across his hideous scars.

'I am not as the Fox. My tongue is frozen like the river. I cannot make great talk. My words are few. The Fox says great deeds are afoot this night. Good! Talk flows from his tongue like the freshets of the spring, but he is chary of deeds. This night shall I do battle with the Wolf. I shall slay him, and Zarinska shall sit by my fire. The Bear has spoken.'

Though pandemonium raged about him, 'Scruff' Mackenzie held his ground. Aware how useless was the rifle at close quarters, he slipped both holsters to the fore, ready for action, and drew his mittens till his hands were barely shielded by the elbow gauntlets. He knew there was no hope in attack en masse, but true to his boast, was prepared to die with teeth fast-locked. But the Bear restrained his comrades, beating back the more impetuous with his terrible fist. As the tumult began to die away, Mackenzie shot a glance in the direction of Zarinska. It was a superb picture. She was leaning forward on her snowshoes, lips apart and nostrils quivering, like a tigress about to spring. Her great black eyes were fixed upon her tribesmen, in fear and defiance. So extreme the tension, she had forgotten to breathe. With one hand pressed spasmodically against her breast and the other as tightly gripped about the dog-whip, she was as turned to stone. Even as he looked, relief came to her. Her muscles loosened; with a heavy sigh she settled back, giving him a look of more than love—of worship.

Thling-Tinneh was trying to speak, but his people drowned his voice. Then Mackenzie strode forward. The Fox opened his mouth to a piercing yell, but so savagely did Mackenzie whirl upon him that he shrank back, his larynx all agurgle with suppressed sound. His discomfiture was greeted with roars of laughter, and served to soothe his fellows to a listening mood.

'Brothers! The White Man, whom ye have chosen to call the Wolf, came among you with fair words. He was not like the Inuit; he spoke not lies. He came as a friend, as one who would be a brother. But your men have had their say, and the time for soft words is past. First, I will tell you that the Shaman has an evil tongue and is a false prophet, that the messages he spake are not those of the Fire-Bringer. His ears are locked to the voice of the Raven, and out of his own head he weaves cunning fancies, and he has made fools of you. He has no power. When the dogs were killed and eaten, and your stomachs were heavy with untanned hide and strips of moccasins; when the old men died, and the old women died, and the babes at the dry dugs of the mothers died; when the land was dark, and ye perished as do the salmon in the fall; aye, when the famine was upon you, did the Shaman bring reward to your hunters? Did the Shaman put meat in your bellies? Again I say, the Shaman is without power. Thus I spit upon his face!'

Though taken aback by the sacrilege, there was no uproar. Some of the women were even frightened, but among the men there was an uplifting, as though in preparation or anticipation of the miracle. All eyes were turned upon the two central figures. The priest realized the crucial moment, felt his power tottering, opened his mouth in denunciation, but fled backward before the truculent advance, upraised fist, and flashing eyes, of Mackenzie. He sneered and resumed.

'Was I stricken dead? Did the lightning burn me? Did the stars fall from the sky and crush me? Pish! I have done with the dog. Now will I tell you of my people, who are the mightiest of all the peoples, who rule in all the lands. At first we hunt as I hunt, alone. After that we hunt in packs; and at last, like the caribou-run, we sweep across all the land. Those whom we take into our lodges live; those who will not come die. Zarinska is a comely maiden, full and strong, fit to become the mother of Wolves. Though I die, such shall she become; for my brothers are many, and they will follow the scent of my dogs. Listen to the Law of the Wolf: Whoso taketh the life of one Wolf, the forfeit shall ten of his people pay. In many lands has the price been paid; in many lands shall it yet be paid.

'Now will I deal with the Fox and the Bear. It seems they have cast eyes upon the maiden. So? Behold, I have bought her! Thling-Tinneh leans upon the rifle; the goods of purchase are by his fire. Yet will I be fair to the young men. To the Fox, whose tongue is dry with many words, will I give of tobacco five long plugs. Thus will his mouth be wetted that he may make much noise in the council. But to the Bear, of whom I am well proud, will I give of blankets two; of flour, twenty cups; of tobacco, double that of the Fox; and if he fare with me over the Mountains of the East, then will I give him a rifle, mate to Thling-Tinneh's. If not? Good! The Wolf is weary of speech. Yet once again will he say the Law: Whoso taketh the life of one Wolf, the forfeit shall ten of his people pay.'

Mackenzie smiled as he stepped back to his old position, but at heart he was full of trouble. The night was yet dark. The girl came to his side, and he listened closely as she told of the Bear's battle-tricks with the knife.

The decision was for war. In a trice, scores of moccasins were widening the space of beaten snow by the fire. There was much chatter about the seeming defeat of the Shaman; some averred he had but withheld his power, while others conned past events and agreed with the Wolf. The Bear came to the centre of the battle-ground, a long naked hunting-knife of Russian make in his hand. The Fox called attention to Mackenzie's revolvers; so he stripped his belt, buckling it about Zarinska, into whose hands he also entrusted his rifle. She shook her head that she could not shoot,—small chance had a woman to handle such precious things.

'Then, if danger come by my back, cry aloud, 'My husband!' No; thus, 'My husband!'"'

He laughed as she repeated it, pinched her cheek, and re-entered the circle. Not only in reach and stature had the Bear the advantage of him, but his blade was longer by a good two inches. 'Scruff' Mackenzie had looked into the eyes of men before, and he knew it was a man who stood against him; yet he quickened to the glint of light on the steel, to the dominant pulse of his race.

Time and again he was forced to the edge of the fire or the deep snow, and time and again, with the foot tactics of the pugilist, he worked back to the centre. Not a voice was lifted in encouragement, while his antagonist was heartened with applause, suggestions, and warnings. But his teeth only shut the tighter as the knives clashed together, and he thrust or eluded with a coolness born of conscious strength. At first he felt compassion for his enemy; but this fled before the primal instinct of life, which in turn gave way to the lust of slaughter. The ten thousand years of culture fell from him, and he was a cave-dweller, doing battle for his female.

Twice he pricked the Bear, getting away unscathed; but the third time caught, and to save himself, free hands closed on fighting hands, and they came together. Then did he realize the tremendous strength of his opponent. His muscles were knotted in painful lumps, and cords and tendons threatened to snap with the strain; yet nearer and nearer came the Russian steel. He tried to break away, but only weakened himself. The fur-clad circle closed in, certain of and anxious to see the final stroke. But with wrestler's trick, swinging partly to the side, he struck at his adversary with his head. Involuntarily the Bear leaned back, disturbing his centre of gravity. Simultaneous with this, Mackenzie tripped properly and threw his whole weight forward, hurling him clear through the circle into the deep snow. The Bear floundered out and came back full tilt.

'O my husband!' Zarinska's voice rang out, vibrant with danger.

To the twang of a bowstring, Mackenzie swept low to the ground, and a bone-barbed arrow passed over him into the breast of the Bear, whose momentum carried him over his crouching foe. The next instant Mackenzie was up and about. The Bear lay motionless, but across the fire was the Shaman, drawing a second arrow.

Mackenzie's knife leaped short in the air. He caught the heavy blade by the point. There was a flash of light as it spanned the fire. Then the Shaman, the hilt alone appearing without his throat, swayed and pitched forward into the glowing embers.

Click! Click!—the Fox had possessed himself of Thling-Tinneh's rifle and was vainly trying to throw a shell into place. But he dropped it at the sound of Mackenzie's laughter.

'So the Fox has not learned the way of the plaything? He is yet a woman. Come! Bring it, that I may show thee!'

The Fox hesitated.

'Come, I say!'

He slouched forward like a beaten cur.

'Thus, and thus; so the thing is done.' A shell flew into place and the trigger was at cock as Mackenzie brought it to shoulder.

'The Fox has said great deeds were afoot this night, and he spoke true. There have been great deeds, yet least among them were those of the Fox. Is he still intent to take Zarinska to his lodge? Is he minded to tread the trail already broken by the Shaman and the Bear? No? Good!'

Mackenzie turned contemptuously and drew his knife from the priest's throat.

'Are any of the young men so minded? If so, the Wolf will take them by two and three till none are left. No? Good! Thling-Tinneh, I now give thee this rifle a second time. If, in the days to come, thou shouldst journey to the Country of the Yukon, know thou that there shall always be a place and much food by the fire of the Wolf. The night is now passing into the day. I go, but I may come again. And for the last time, remember the Law of the Wolf!'

He was supernatural in their sight as he rejoined Zarinska. She took her place at the head of the team, and the dogs swung into motion. A few moments later they were swallowed up by the ghostly forest. Till now Mackenzie had waited; he slipped into his snowshoes to follow.

'Has the Wolf forgotten the five long plugs?'

Mackenzie turned upon the Fox angrily; then the humour of it struck him.

'I will give thee one short plug.'

'As the Wolf sees fit,' meekly responded the Fox, stretching out his hand.

11

THE WIFE OF A KING

Once when the Northland was very young, the social and civic virtues were remarkably alike for their paucity and their simplicity. When the burden of domestic duties grew grievous, and the fireside mood expanded to a constant protest against its bleak loneliness, the adventurers from the Southland, in lieu of better, paid the stipulated prices and took unto themselves native wives. It was a foretaste of Paradise to the women, for it must be confessed that the white rovers gave far better care and treatment of them than did their Indian copartners. Of course, the white men themselves were satisfied with such deals, as were also the Indian men for that matter. Having sold their daughters and sisters for cotton blankets and obsolete rifles and traded their warm furs for flimsy calico and bad whisky, the sons of the soil promptly and cheerfully succumbed to quick consumption and other swift diseases correlated with the blessings of a superior civilization.

It was in these days of Arcadian simplicity that Cal Galbraith journeyed through the land and fell sick on the Lower River. It was a refreshing advent in the lives of the good Sisters of the Holy Cross, who gave him shelter and medicine; though they little dreamed of the hot elixir infused into his veins by the touch of their soft hands and their gentle ministrations. Cal Galbraith became troubled with strange thoughts which clamoured for attention till he laid eyes on the Mission girl, Madeline. Yet he gave no sign, biding his time patiently. He strengthened with the coming spring, and when the sun rode the heavens in a golden circle, and the joy and throb of life was in all the land, he gathered his still weak body together and departed.

Now, Madeline, the Mission girl, was an orphan. Her white father had failed to give a bald-faced grizzly the trail one day, and had died quickly. Then her Indian mother, having no man to fill the winter cache, had tried the hazardous experiment of waiting till the salmon-run on fifty pounds of flour and half as many of bacon. After that, the baby, Chook-ra, went to live with the good Sisters, and to be thenceforth known by another name.

But Madeline still had kinsfolk, the nearest being a dissolute uncle who outraged his vitals with inordinate quantities of the white man's whisky. He strove daily to walk with the gods, and incidentally, his feet sought shorter trails to the grave. When sober he suffered exquisite torture. He had no conscience. To this ancient vagabond Cal Galbraith duly presented himself, and they consumed many words and much tobacco in the conversation that followed. Promises were also made; and in the end the old heathen took a few pounds of dried salmon and his birch-bark canoe, and paddled away to the Mission of the Holy Cross.

It is not given the world to know what promises he made and what lies he told—the Sisters never gossip; but when he returned, upon his swarthy chest there was a brass crucifix, and in his canoe his niece Madeline. That night there was a grand wedding and a potlach; so that for two days to follow there was no fishing done by the village. But in the morning Madeline shook the dust of the Lower River from her moccasins, and with her husband, in a poling-boat, went to live on the Upper River in a place known as the Lower Country. And in the years which followed she was a good wife, sharing her husband's hardships and cooking his food. And she kept him in straight trails, till he learned to save his dust and to work mightily. In the end, he struck it rich and built a cabin in Circle City; and his happiness was such that men who came to visit him in his home-circle became restless at the sight of it and envied him greatly.

But the Northland began to mature and social amenities to make their appearance. Hitherto, the Southland had sent forth its sons; but it now belched forth a new exodus—this time of its daughters. Sisters and wives they were not; but they did not fail to put new ideas in the heads of the men, and to elevate the tone of things in ways peculiarly their own. No more did the squaws gather at the dances, go roaring down the centre in the good, old Virginia reels, or make merry with jolly 'Dan Tucker'. They fell back on their natural stoicism and uncomplainingly watched the rule of their white sisters from their cabins.

Then another exodus came over the mountains from the prolific Southland. This time it was of women that became mighty in the land. Their word was law; their law was steel. They frowned upon the Indian wives, while the other women became mild and walked humbly. There were cowards who became ashamed of their ancient covenants with the daughters of the soil, who looked with a new distaste upon their dark-skinned children; but there were also others—men—who remained true and proud of their aboriginal vows. When it became the fashion to divorce the native wives. Cal Galbraith retained his manhood, and in so doing felt the heavy hand of the women who had come last, knew least, but who ruled the land.

One day, the Upper Country, which lies far above Circle City, was pronounced rich. Dog-teams carried the news to Salt Water; golden argosies freighted the lure across the North Pacific; wires and cables sang with the tidings; and the world heard for the first time of the Klondike River and the Yukon Country.

Cal Galbraith had lived the years quietly. He had been a good husband to Madeline, and she had blessed him. But somehow discontent fell upon him; he felt vague yearnings for his own kind, for the life he had been shut out from—a general sort of desire, which men sometimes feel, to break out and taste the prime of living. Besides, there drifted down the river wild rumours of the wonderful El Dorado, glowing descriptions of the city of logs and tents, and ludicrous accounts of the che-cha-quas who had rushed in and were stampeding the whole country. Circle City was dead. The world had moved on upriver and become a new and most marvellous world.

Cal Galbraith grew restless on the edge of things, and wished to see with his own eyes. So, after the wash-up, he weighed in a couple of hundred pounds of dust on the Company's big scales, and took a draft for the same on Dawson. Then he put Tom Dixon in charge of his mines, kissed Madeline goodbye, promised to be back before the first mush-ice ran, and took passage on an upriver steamer.

Madeline waited, waited through all the three months of daylight. She fed the dogs, gave much of her time to Young Cal, watched the short summer fade away and the sun begin its long journey to the south. And she prayed much in the manner of the Sisters of the Holy Cross. The fall came, and with it there was mush-ice on the Yukon, and Circle City kings returning to the winter's work at their mines, but no Cal Galbraith. Tom Dixon received a letter, however, for his men sledded up her winter's supply of dry pine. The Company received a letter for its dog-teams filled her cache with their best provisions, and she was told that her credit was limitless.

Through all the ages man has been held the chief instigator of the woes of woman; but in this case the men held their tongues and swore harshly at one of their number who was away, while the women failed utterly to emulate them. So, without needless delay, Madeline heard strange tales of Cal Galbraith's doings; also, of a certain Greek dancer who played with men as children did with bubbles. Now Madeline was an Indian woman, and further, she had no woman friend to whom to go for wise counsel. She prayed and planned by turns, and that night, being quick of resolve and action, she harnessed the dogs, and with Young Cal securely lashed to the sled, stole away.

Though the Yukon still ran free, the eddy-ice was growing, and each day saw the river dwindling to a slushy thread. Save him who has done the like, no man may know what she endured in travelling a hundred miles on the rim-ice; nor may they understand the toil and hardship of breaking the two hundred miles of packed ice which remained after the river froze for good. But Madeline was an Indian woman, so she did these things, and one night there came a knock at Malemute Kid's door. Thereat he fed a team of starving dogs, put a healthy youngster to bed, and turned his attention to the exhausted woman. He removed her ice-bound moccasins while he listened to her tale, and stuck the point of his knife into her feet that he might see how far they were frozen.

Despite his tremendous virility, Malemute Kid was possessed of a softer, womanly element, which could win the confidence of a snarling wolf-dog or draw confessions from the most wintry heart. Nor did he seek them. Hearts opened to him as spontaneously as flowers to the sun. Even the priest, Father Roubeau, had been known to confess to him, while the men and women of the Northland were ever knocking at his door—a door from which the latch-string hung always out. To Madeline, he could do no wrong, make no mistake. She had known him from the time she first cast her lot among the people of her father's race; and to her half-barbaric mind it seemed that in him was centred the wisdom of the ages, that between his vision and the future there could be no intervening veil.

There were false ideals in the land. The social strictures of Dawson were not synonymous with those of the previous era, and the swift maturity of the Northland involved much wrong.

Malemute Kid was aware of this, and he had Cal Galbraith's measure accurately. He knew a hasty word was the father of much evil; besides, he was minded to teach a great lesson and bring shame upon the man. So Stanley Prince, the young mining expert, was called into the conference the following night as was also Lucky Jack Harrington and his violin. That same night, Bettles, who owed a great debt to Malemute Kid, harnessed up Cal Galbraith's dogs, lashed Cal Galbraith, Junior, to the sled, and slipped away in the dark for Stuart River.

II

'So; one—two—three, one—two—three. Now reverse! No, no! Start up again, Jack. See—this way.' Prince executed the movement as one should who has led the cotillion.

'Now; one—two—three, one—two—three. Reverse! Ah! that's better. Try it again. I say, you know, you mustn't look at your feet. One—two—three, one—two—three. Shorter steps! You are not hanging to the gee-pole just now. Try it over. There! that's the way. One—two—three, one—two—three.'

Round and round went Prince and Madeline in an interminable waltz. The table and stools had been shoved over against the wall to increase the room. Malemute Kid sat on the bunk, chin to knees, greatly interested. Jack Harrington sat beside him, scraping away on his violin and following the dancers.

It was a unique situation, the undertaking of these three men with the woman. The most pathetic part, perhaps, was the businesslike way in which they went about it. No athlete was ever trained more rigidly for a coming contest, nor wolf-dog for the harness, than was she. But they had good material, for Madeline, unlike most women of her race, in her childhood had escaped the carrying of heavy burdens and the toil of the trail. Besides, she was a clean-limbed, willowy creature, possessed of much grace which had not hitherto been realized. It was this grace which the men strove to bring out and knock into shape.

'Trouble with her she learned to dance all wrong,' Prince remarked to the bunk after having deposited his breathless pupil on the table. 'She's quick at picking up; yet I could do better had she never danced a step. But say, Kid, I can't understand this.' Prince imitated a peculiar movement of the shoulders and head—a weakness Madeline suffered from in walking.

'Lucky for her she was raised in the Mission,' Malemute Kid answered. 'Packing, you know—the head-strap. Other Indian women have it bad, but she didn't do any packing till after she married, and then only at first. Saw hard lines with that husband of hers. They went through the Forty-Mile famine together.'

'But can we break it?'

'Don't know. Perhaps long walks with her trainers will make the riffle. Anyway, they'll take it out some, won't they, Madeline?'

The girl nodded assent. If Malemute Kid, who knew all things, said so, why it was so. That was all there was about it.

She had come over to them, anxious to begin again. Harrington surveyed her in quest of her points much in the same manner men usually do horses. It certainly was not disappointing, for he asked with sudden interest, 'What did that beggarly uncle of yours get anyway?'

'One rifle, one blanket, twenty bottles of hooch. Rifle broke.' She said this last scornfully, as though disgusted at how low her maiden-value had been rated.

She spoke fair English, with many peculiarities of her husband's speech, but there was still perceptible the Indian accent, the traditional groping after strange gutturals. Even this her instructors had taken in hand, and with no small success, too.

At the next intermission, Prince discovered a new predicament. 'I say, Kid,' he said, 'we're wrong, all wrong. She can't learn in moccasins. Put her feet into slippers, and then onto that waxed floor—phew!'

Madeline raised a foot and regarded her shapeless house-moccasins dubiously. In previous winters, both at Circle City and Forty-Mile, she had danced many a night away with similar footgear, and there had been nothing the matter.

But now—well, if there was anything wrong it was for Malemute Kid to know, not her.

But Malemute Kid did know, and he had a good eye for measures; so he put on his cap and mittens and went down the hill to pay Mrs Eppingwell a call. Her husband, Clove Eppingwell, was prominent in the community as one of the great Government officials. The Kid had noted her slender little foot one night, at the Governor's Ball. And as he also knew her to be as sensible as she was pretty, it was no task to ask of her a certain small favour.

On his return, Madeline withdrew for a moment to the inner room. When she reappeared Prince was startled.

'By Jove!' he gasped. 'Who'd a thought it! The little witch! Why my sister—'

'Is an English girl,' interrupted Malemute Kid, 'with an English foot. This girl comes of a small-footed race. Moccasins just broadened her feet healthily, while she did not misshape them by running with the dogs in her childhood.'

But this explanation failed utterly to allay Prince's admiration. Harrington's commercial instinct was touched, and as he looked upon the exquisitely turned foot and ankle, there ran through his mind the sordid list—'One rifle, one blanket, twenty bottles of hooch.'

Madeline was the wife of a king, a king whose yellow treasure could buy outright a score of fashion's puppets; yet in all her life her feet had known no gear save red-tanned moosehide. At first she had looked in awe at the tiny white-satin slippers; but she had quickly understood the admiration which shone, manlike, in the eyes of the men. Her face flushed with pride. For the moment she was drunken with her woman's loveliness; then she murmured, with increased scorn, 'And one rifle, broke!'

So the training went on. Every day Malemute Kid led the girl out on long walks devoted to the correction of her carriage and the shortening of her stride. There was little likelihood of her identity being discovered, for Cal Galbraith and the rest of the Old-Timers were like lost children among the many strangers who had rushed into the land. Besides, the frost of the North has a bitter tongue, and the tender women of the South, to shield their cheeks from its biting caresses, were prone to the use of canvas masks. With faces obscured and bodies lost in squirrel-skin parkas, a mother and daughter, meeting on trail, would pass as strangers.

The coaching progressed rapidly. At first it had been slow, but later a sudden acceleration had manifested itself. This began from the moment Madeline tried on the white-satin slippers, and in so doing found herself. The pride of her renegade father, apart from any natural self-esteem she might possess, at that instant received its birth. Hitherto, she had deemed herself a woman of an alien breed, of inferior stock, purchased by her lord's favour. Her husband had seemed to her a god, who had lifted her, through no essential virtues on her part, to his own godlike level. But she had never forgotten, even when Young Cal was born, that she was not of his people. As he had been a god, so had his womenkind been goddesses. She might have contrasted herself with them, but she had never compared. It might have been that familiarity bred contempt; however, be that as it may, she had ultimately come to understand these roving white men, and to weigh them. True, her mind was dark to deliberate analysis, but she yet possessed her woman's clarity of vision in such matters. On the night of the slippers she had measured the bold, open admiration of her three man-friends; and for the first time comparison had suggested itself. It was only a foot and an ankle, but—but comparison could not, in the nature of things, cease at that point. She judged herself by their standards till the divinity of her white sisters was shattered. After all, they were only women, and why should she not exalt herself to their midst? In doing these things she learned where she lacked and with the knowledge of her weakness came her strength. And so mightily did she strive that her three trainers often marvelled late into the night over the eternal mystery of woman.

In this way Thanksgiving Night drew near. At irregular intervals Bettles sent word down from Stuart River regarding the welfare of Young Cal. The time of their return was approaching. More than once a casual caller, hearing dance-music and the rhythmic pulse of feet, entered, only to find Harrington scraping away and the other two beating time or arguing noisily over a mooted step. Madeline was never in evidence, having precipitately fled to the inner room.

On one of these nights Cal Galbraith dropped in. Encouraging news had just come down from Stuart River, and Madeline had surpassed herself—not in walk alone, and carriage and grace, but in womanly roguishness. They had indulged in sharp repartee and she had defended herself brilliantly; and then, yielding to the intoxication of the moment, and of her own power, she had bullied, and mastered, and wheedled, and patronized them with most astonishing success. And instinctively, involuntarily, they had bowed, not to her beauty, her wisdom, her wit, but to that indefinable something in woman to which man yields yet cannot name. The room was dizzy with sheer delight as she and Prince whirled through the last dance of the evening. Harrington was throwing in inconceivable flourishes, while Malemute Kid, utterly abandoned, had seized the broom and was executing mad gyrations on his own account.

At this instant the door shook with a heavy rap-rap, and their quick glances noted the lifting of the latch. But they had survived similar situations before. Harrington never broke a note. Madeline shot through the waiting door to the inner room. The broom went hurtling under the bunk, and by the time Cal Galbraith and Louis

Savoy got their heads in, Malemute Kid and Prince were in each other's arms, wildly schottisching down the room.

As a rule, Indian women do not make a practice of fainting on provocation, but Madeline came as near to it as she ever had in her life. For an hour she crouched on the floor, listening to the heavy voices of the men rumbling up and down in mimic thunder. Like familiar chords of childhood melodies, every intonation, every trick of her husband's voice swept in upon her, fluttering her heart and weakening her knees till she lay half-fainting against the door. It was well she could neither see nor hear when he took his departure.

'When do you expect to go back to Circle City?' Malemute Kid asked simply.

'Haven't thought much about it,' he replied. 'Don't think till after the ice breaks.'

'And Madeline?'

He flushed at the question, and there was a quick droop to his eyes. Malemute Kid could have despised him for that, had he known men less. As it was, his gorge rose against the wives and daughters who had come into the land, and not satisfied with usurping the place of the native women, had put unclean thoughts in the heads of the men and made them ashamed.

'I guess she's all right,' the Circle City King answered hastily, and in an apologetic manner. 'Tom Dixon's got charge of my interests, you know, and he sees to it that she has everything she wants.'

Malemute Kid laid hand upon his arm and hushed him suddenly. They had stepped without. Overhead, the aurora, a gorgeous wanton, flaunted miracles of colour; beneath lay the sleeping town. Far below, a solitary dog gave tongue. The King again began to speak, but the Kid pressed his hand for silence. The sound multiplied. Dog after dog took up the strain till the full-throated chorus swayed the night. To him who hears for the first time this weird song, is told the first and greatest secret of the Northland; to him who has heard it often, it is the solemn knell of lost endeavour. It is the plaint of tortured souls, for in it is invested the heritage of the North, the suffering of countless generations—the warning and the requiem to the world's estrays.

Cal Galbraith shivered slightly as it died away in half-caught sobs. The Kid read his thoughts openly, and wandered back with him through all the weary days of famine and disease; and with him was also the patient Madeline, sharing his pains and perils, never doubting, never complaining. His mind's retina vibrated to a score of pictures, stern, clear-cut, and the hand of the past drew back with heavy fingers on his heart. It was the psychological moment. Malemute Kid was half-tempted to play his reserve card and win the game; but the lesson was too mild as yet, and he let it pass. The next instant they had gripped hands, and the King's beaded moccasins were drawing protests from the outraged snow as he crunched down the hill.

Madeline in collapse was another woman to the mischievous creature of an hour before, whose laughter had been so infectious and whose heightened colour and flashing eyes had made her teachers for the while forget. Weak and nerveless, she sat in the chair just as she had been dropped there by Prince and Harrington. Malemute Kid frowned. This would never do. When the time of meeting her husband came to hand, she must carry things off with high-handed imperiousness. It was very necessary she should do it after the manner of white women, else the victory would be no victory at all. So he talked to her, sternly, without mincing of words, and initiated her into the weaknesses of his own sex, till she came to understand what simpletons men were after all, and why the word of their women was law.

A few days before Thanksgiving Night, Malemute Kid made another call on Mrs Eppingwell. She promptly overhauled her feminine fripperies, paid a protracted visit to the dry-goods department of the P.C. Company, and returned with the Kid to make Madeline's acquaintance. After that came a period such as the cabin had never seen before, and what with cutting, and fitting, and basting, and stitching, and numerous other wonderful and unknowable things, the male conspirators were more often banished from the premises than not. At such times the Opera House opened its double storm-doors to them. So often did they put their heads together, and so deeply did they drink to curious toasts, that the loungers scented unknown creeks of incalculable richness, and it is known that several che-cha-quas and at least one Old-Timer kept their stampeding packs stored behind the bar, ready to hit the trail at a moment's notice.

Mrs Eppingwell was a woman of capacity; so, when she turned Madeline over to her trainers on Thanksgiving Night she was so transformed that they were almost afraid of her. Prince wrapped a Hudson Bay blanket about her with a mock reverence more real than feigned, while Malemute Kid, whose arm she had taken, found it a severe trial to resume his wonted mentorship. Harrington, with the list of purchases still running through his head, dragged along in the rear, nor opened his mouth once all the way down into the town. When they came to the back door of the Opera House they took the blanket from Madeline's shoulders and spread it on the snow. Slipping out of Prince's moccasins, she stepped upon it in new satin slippers. The masquerade was at its height. She hesitated, but they jerked open the door and shoved her in. Then they ran around to come in by the front entrance.

III

'Where is Freda?' the Old-Timers questioned, while the che-cha-quas were equally energetic in asking who Freda was. The ballroom buzzed with her name. It was on everybody's lips. Grizzled 'sourdough boys', day-labourers at the mines but proud of their degree, either patronized the spruce-looking tenderfeet and lied eloquently—the 'sourdough boys' being specially created to toy with truth—or gave them savage looks of indignation because of their ignorance. Perhaps forty kings of the Upper and Lower Countries were on the floor, each deeming himself hot on the trail and sturdily backing his judgment with the yellow dust of the realm. An assistant was sent to the man at the scales, upon whom had fallen the burden of weighing up the sacks, while several of the gamblers, with the rules of chance at their finger-ends, made up alluring books on the field and favourites.

Which was Freda? Time and again the 'Greek Dancer' was thought to have been discovered, but each discovery brought panic to the betting ring and a frantic registering of new wagers by those who wished to hedge. Malemute Kid took an interest in the hunt, his advent being hailed uproariously by the revellers, who knew him to a man. The Kid had a good eye for the trick of a step, and ear for the lilt of a voice, and his private choice was a marvellous creature who scintillated as the 'Aurora Borealis'. But the Greek dancer was too subtle for even his penetration. The majority of the gold-hunters seemed to have centred their verdict on the 'Russian Princess', who was the most graceful in the room, and hence could be no other than Freda Moloof.

During a quadrille a roar of satisfaction went up. She was discovered. At previous balls, in the figure, 'all hands round', Freda had displayed an inimitable step and variation peculiarly her own. As the figure was called, the 'Russian Princess' gave the unique rhythm to limb and body. A chorus of I-told-you-so's shook the squared roof-beams, when lo! it was noticed that 'Aurora Borealis' and another masque, the 'Spirit of the Pole', were performing the same trick equally well. And when two twin 'Sun-Dogs' and a 'Frost Queen' followed suit, a second assistant was dispatched to the aid of the man at the scales.

Bettles came off trail in the midst of the excitement, descending upon them in a hurricane of frost. His rimed brows turned to cataracts as he whirled about; his moustache, still frozen, seemed gemmed with diamonds and turned the light in varicoloured rays; while the flying feet slipped on the chunks of ice which rattled from his moccasins and German socks. A Northland dance is quite an informal affair, the men of the creeks and trails having lost whatever fastidiousness they might have at one time possessed; and only in the high official circles are conventions at all observed. Here, caste carried no significance. Millionaires and paupers, dog-drivers and mounted policemen joined hands with 'ladies in the centre', and swept around the circle performing most remarkable capers. Primitive in their pleasure, boisterous and rough, they displayed no rudeness, but rather a crude chivalry more genuine than the most polished courtesy.

In his quest for the 'Greek Dancer', Cal Galbraith managed to get into the same set with the 'Russian Princess', toward whom popular suspicion had turned. But by the time he had guided her through one dance, he was willing not only to stake his millions that she was not Freda, but that he had had his arm about her waist before. When or where he could not tell, but the puzzling sense of familiarity so wrought upon him that he turned his attention to the discovery of her identity. Malemute Kid might have aided him instead of occasionally taking the Princess for a few turns and talking earnestly to her in low tones. But it was Jack Harrington who paid the 'Russian Princess' the most assiduous court. Once he drew Cal Galbraith aside and hazarded wild guesses as to who she was, and explained to him that he was going in to win. That rankled the Circle City King, for man is not by nature monogamic, and he forgot both Madeline and Freda in the new quest.

It was soon noised about that the 'Russian Princess' was not Freda Moloof. Interest deepened. Here was a fresh enigma. They knew Freda though they could not find her, but here was somebody they had found and did not know. Even the women could not place her, and they knew every good dancer in the camp. Many took her for one of the official clique, indulging in a silly escapade.

Not a few asserted she would disappear before the unmasking. Others were equally positive that she was the woman reporter of the *Kansas City Star*, come to write them up at ninety dollars per column. And the men at the scales worked busily.

At one o'clock every couple took to the floor. The unmasking began amid laughter and delight, like that of carefree children. There was no end of Oh's and Ah's as mask after mask was lifted. The scintillating 'Aurora Borealis' became the brawny negress whose income from washing the community's clothes ran at about five hundred a month. The twin 'Sun-Dogs' discovered moustaches on their upper lips, and were recognized as brother Fraction-Kings of El Dorado. In one of the most prominent sets, and the slowest in uncovering, was Cal Galbraith with the 'Spirit of the Pole'. Opposite him was Jack Harrington and the 'Russian Princess'. The rest had discovered themselves, yet the 'Greek Dancer' was still missing. All eyes were upon the group. Cal Galbraith, in response to their cries, lifted his partner's mask. Freda's wonderful face and brilliant eyes flashed out upon them. A roar went up, to be squelched suddenly in the new and absorbing mystery of the 'Russian Princess'. Her face was still hidden, and Jack Harrington was struggling with her. The dancers tittered on the tiptoes of expectancy. He crushed her dainty costume roughly, and then—and then the revellers exploded. The joke was on them. They had danced all night with a tabooed native woman.

But those that knew, and they were many, ceased abruptly, and a hush fell upon the room. Cal Galbraith crossed over with great strides, angrily, and spoke to Madeline in polyglot Chinook. But she retained her composure, apparently oblivious to the fact that she was the cynosure of all eyes, and answered him in English. She showed neither fright nor anger, and Malemute Kid chuckled at her well-bred equanimity. The King felt baffled, defeated; his common Siwash wife had passed beyond him.

'Come!' he said finally. 'Come on home.'

'I beg pardon,' she replied; 'I have agreed to go to supper with Mr Harrington. Besides, there's no end of dances promised.'

Harrington extended his arm to lead her away. He evinced not the slightest disinclination toward showing his back, but Malemute Kid had by this time edged in closer. The Circle City King was stunned. Twice his hand dropped to his belt, and twice the Kid gathered himself to spring; but the retreating couple passed through the supper-room door where canned oysters were spread at five dollars the plate. The crowd sighed audibly, broke up into couples, and followed them. Freda pouted and went in with Cal Galbraith; but she had a good heart and a sure tongue, and she spoiled his oysters for him. What she said is of no importance, but his face went red and white at intervals, and he swore repeatedly and savagely at himself.

The supper-room was filled with a pandemonium of voices, which ceased suddenly as Cal Galbraith stepped over to his wife's table. Since the unmasking considerable weights of dust had been placed as to the outcome. Everybody watched with breathless interest. Harrington's blue eyes were steady, but under the overhanging tablecloth a Smith & Wesson balanced on his knee. Madeline looked up, casually, with little interest.

'May—may I have the next round dance with you?' the King stuttered.

The wife of the King glanced at her card and inclined her head.

ABOUT TERRY O'BRIEN

Terry O'Brien is an academic with three decades of experience in teaching language and communication skills in India and abroad. He also headed a college under the auspices of the University of Delhi.

A prolific writer, with several books to his credit, Terry O'Brien is a reputed professional motivational speaker and a quizmaster.